I0626259

STARVED

JANE THORNTON, BOOK 2

C.E. BLACK

This is a work of fiction. Names, characters, places, and incidents either are the product of the author's imagination or are used fictitiously. Any resemblance to actual persons, living or dead, business establishments, events or locales is entirely coincidental.

STARVED

Copyright © 2017 by C.E. Black

Cover Design by C.E. Black

Editor: Kimberly Gallant

For information: authorceblack@ceblack.org

ISBN: 978-0-9987885-5-5

Printed in the United States of America

JANE THORNTON TRILOGY
BY C.E. BLACK

"There's safety in pairs, but three is better."

HUNGER
STARVED
SATED

1

"JANE. JANE, HONEY, IT'S TIME TO GET UP."

With a pounding heart, my eyelids fluttered open at the familiar voice. A voice I'd painfully missed and would never hear again outside of my dreams. Which was how I realized immediately that I was dreaming. A dream I knew all too well. Though the warm, feminine voice had sounded as if it'd been spoken right next to my ear, it had actually come from downstairs in the kitchen.

I climbed from the bed, shivering as cold air swept across my skin, and hurried to the stairs. The peeling floral wallpaper blurred in my peripheral vision causing me confusion. Instead of the oak from my childhood home, cream paint coated the wooden railing beneath my fingertips and a glance at my bare feet on uncarpeted stairs showed me why I felt so cold. This wasn't my old house. This was the home me and Annabelle were living in.

The location of the dream had changed, but would the rest? Would the owner of the voice be here?

One of my questions was answered when I found my

mother, her back to me, humming a meaningless tune as she stood in front of the stove. Internally, I sighed with relief that at least that part of the dream had not changed. This was the only portion I looked forward to every night. A chance to see her again.

Her long silver hair had been pulled into a neat bun at the nape of her neck. She'd gone prematurely gray in her late twenties, and I had a clear memory of her threatening to dye it on many occasions, but my father would beg her not to, telling her how much he loved it just the way it was. She'd blush, slapping his arm as if he were joking. But she had never used a single drop of dye. Not even after he'd passed.

"Jane. Are you ready?" she asked without turning away from the stove.

This part of the dream was a memory. It had been the first day at my new job. I wasn't sure why my brain had decided to put that particular conversation on repeat. There'd been nothing special about it—only the same discussion I'd had with her several times over the course of my life.

Instead of answering, I watched her, my anxiety growing as she asked me questions. *Where would I eat lunch? When would I be home?* It wasn't that I didn't want to answer them, it was that I couldn't. I was just an observer in this dream. But I soaked in her presence…her voice…because I knew this dream would take a turn for the worse. Already, the cold seeped into my bones. I could see my breath in front of my face as the temperature dropped.

"Don't be upset with her. She only wants what's best for you."

I turned to my father who sat at the dining room table reading a newspaper. His skin was pale and his lips were tinged blue. By now his sandy-colored hair should have been streaked with gray, but he'd still been young when he died. I'd only been eight years old at the time.

His words had been out of context, but it was something I'd heard him say many times during my childhood.

I wanted to go to him, or at the very least stare at him a little longer. But I had no control of my body, and my heart twisted with sorrow as my head turned away. My eyes were immediately drawn to the window where a shadowing figure hovered on the other side of the back door. I sucked in a shaky breath, knowing exactly what was about to happen.

"No," I tried to say, but it only sounded in my head. There was nothing I could do to stop my mother as she opened the back door.

"Well, hello, John," she greeted our neighbor, then gasped as they both fell to the floor in a tangle of arms and legs. John's face was hidden in the crease of my mom's neck, his fingers gripping tightly to her arms as he fed.

This was the scene that would repeatedly play over and over in my mind. She didn't scream. She never screamed. It would be over too quick for that.

I trembled, my body weeping in my sleep as I watched my mother being murdered. The life in her terrified gaze dimmed. It would be over soon. This was the end of it. But as the dream lingered longer than usual, I began to panic for another reason. I should have woken up by now.

Just as the thought crossed my mind, another change happened. The flesh eater pinning my mother to the floor stopped feeding. His head lifted slowly and he sniffed the room as if sensing my presence. My already racing heart picked up speed, bursting with adrenaline as he turned his head in my direction. Would I experience the same fate as my mother? Would he attack while I stood paralyzed? I would have preferred that outcome. Instead, I woke with the image of Mason's dead, milky eyes staring back at me.

Heart galloping, I stared at the ceiling, willing my body to still its trembling and my lungs to take a decent breath. I hadn't woken up so shaken in a long time. I shivered at the memory of my ex-lover's face, his mouth covered in my mother's blood.

I climbed from the bed before I could think more about it. It was just a dream. A dream that wasn't even close to reality. For one, Mason wasn't the one who'd killed my mother. And two, Kaden would have never allowed Mason to turn.

A rush of sadness swallowed me whole. Mason was surely dead by now. It had been weeks since I'd left them. And underneath the grief was also another kind of heartache. Kaden had never come.

After throwing on a pair of jeans, I laced up my boots and headed for the stairs. Halfway down I heard first the sizzle, then the smell of bacon frying in the kitchen. Grinning, I flew down the stairs to reach my newest friend. We had decided to take turns making supply runs, while the other would stay to protect the farm. She'd been gone for three days. I'd known as time went on we'd have to venture farther out than the closest town if we were going to find anything, but it hadn't stopped me from worrying.

"Hey, sleepy head," she said as I rounded the corner.

Five or six candles dotted the table and counter where she worked. Which made me wonder how I was smelling bacon. The stove was hooked to a portable generator. The refrigerator, however, was not.

With her back to me, Annabelle stood in front of the stove, her hips moving side to side as she hummed under her breath a song I'd never heard before. The scene was too much like my dream, causing my stomach to tighten uncomfortably.

"Hey, you okay?" Giving me a concerned look over her shoulder, she turned off the burner and waited.

Instead of answering Annabelle's question, I asked, *"Bacon?"* Her lessons on sign language had been going well, but she was still a little unaccustomed. It could take years for her to become fluent.

Under the table, Poco's tail thumped impatiently against the hardwood floor. Smiling, I bent down to rub behind his ears, receiving doggy kisses on my cheek in return.

"Huh? Oh, no. Canned ham," Annabelle corrected. Holding up the plate, she sent me a wry smile before setting it down on the table next to me. "I got a case of the stuff. It's been a while, but I remember it tasting almost like bacon if you sliced it thin and pan seared it until it gets crispy."

I wasn't so sure about that but I was willing to give it a try. It had to be better than the cold, gelatinous stuff. Sitting down, we both reached for a slice and took identical hesitant bites. I chewed slowly, thoughtfully. It wasn't quite as crispy as I expected. A little chewy.

"Hmm," Annabelle nodded. "Not bad," she said, giving a slice to Poco.

Not bacon. But close enough. And I'd been right. Much better than right out of the can. Before reaching for another piece, I asked where she got our breakfast. That's some luck running across a case of anything. Much less something like canned ham that would last for almost forever.

After watching my hands carefully, Annabelle's face broke out into a wide grin. "I found a few more generators." She waved a hand toward the mud room where three brand new generators were sitting.

I smiled back, ecstatic. We needed at least one more for the well-pump. It was going to be a chore to figure out how to connect it but I was willing to sacrifice the time and frustration. Hauling buckets into the house had gotten old.

I also made a mental note for our next supply run. We were going to need more fuel. So far, we'd been using gasoline. It was pretty easy to find, especially with so many abandoned cars everywhere. But it wouldn't last forever. We would need to come up with an alternative soon.

"I also found people."

Startled by her statement, I choked on the piece of ham I was trying to swallow.

Annabelle jumped from her seat, holding out a bottle of water. "Hey, you okay?" she asked.

Taking the bottle from her hand, I took small sips until my throat cleared, then wasted no time demanding answers. My hands flew as I hounded her for more information. *Where are these people? Are they close? Are you okay? Did they hurt you? Where are they now?*

"Jane, take a deep breath and calm down. I can't understand a thing you're signing. And your face is turning red."

I dropped my fisted hands on the table. *Calm down?* This was serious. Did she have any idea what could happen if someone found us here? Sucking in a breath through my nose, my teeth ground together as I glared at my friend. What had she been thinking?

Annabelle held out both hands, "Okay, okay. Just hear me out."

I nodded once for her to continue. This had better be good.

Instead, she stood from the table. "On the way in, I noticed a piece of the fence needs fixin'. Want to help me? We can talk while we work. I think the walk will do us good."

It took several deep breaths before I was calm enough to think clearly. The way Annabelle had eyed me warily, I could tell my reaction had surprised her, and I didn't like it. She deserved better. I decided to give her the benefit of the doubt and followed her outside.

With each step, the ground crunched beneath our feet as we made our way toward the tree line. The knee-high grass had turned dry and brown and the trees surrounding the clearing where the house sat were bare. Poco ran ahead of us, darting from spot to spot, sniffing his territory for intruders.

Overhead, heavy gray clouds walled up the sky. Snow was coming. It wouldn't be our first snowfall of the season, but we'd had it easy so far. Winter had just begun, and things were bound to get worse. I looked forward to spring. As soon as the ground thawed, we could start a garden.

As we ventured into the woods, Annabelle was unusually quiet. I wanted to ask her again about the people she'd met, but I shoved my gloved fists into my coat pockets and stared straight ahead. I was older than her by only three years. Not old enough to mother the poor woman. At times, I couldn't help it. Though only twenty-six, I sometimes felt like a hundred and twenty-six.

My anxiety began creeping to nuclear levels. If she hadn't spoken by the time we reached the fence, I would ask her again. Annabelle could take care of herself. She was smart, strong, and resourceful. Everything you needed to be in this world. But we were partners now. We had to be able to communicate if we were going to survive.

The bare trees made it easy to see the fence about thirty yards ahead of us. When we'd first walked the property, and found it to be surrounded by a seven-foot-tall chain link fence with brown plastic inserts, we were surprised and relieved. I didn't know why Mason's uncle had decided to protect his property so heavily, but I was grateful. Neither of us knew exactly how large the property was, maybe three or four acres at least. We walked it regularly, looking for damage to the fence or anything out of place.

Not only were we well-protected here, the stove used gas instead of electricity, and there was a working generator. We used it sparingly, though. Also, in the basement, we found jarred food that would definitely come in handy this winter, as well as some root vegetables that looked good. Mason's uncle must have been preparing. And recently. The vegetables looked fairly fresh and the jars only had a light covering of dust on their lids. But where had he gone? My teeth nibbled on my lower lip. I wished I would have asked Mason about him. I wished I'd asked Mason a lot of things.

Annabelle sighed, catching my attention. She wore the same black leather coat she always wore with her arrows hanging from her back in a black quiver that blended with her coat. She carried her bow in her hand at her side. My eyes narrowed disapprovingly at her bare hands. She never wore gloves. I'd tried a billion times to tell her it was getting too cold to spend hours outside without them, but she'd claimed she couldn't shoot well with them. I'd let it go for the time being. But in a month, it was going to be too cold to go without. Unless she wanted to lose a finger or two.

"They were nice," Annabelle said, breaking the silence.

My heart thudded as I looked up to meet her wary eyes.

"I promise, it's not that bad. I saw a group of four, three men and one woman, coming out of a grocery store I was about to check out. I hid and watched them as they loaded up two SUVs with supplies. Then I followed them." She shrugged. "I figured they probably emptied the store anyway."

Head shaking from side to side, I stared at my friend like she was nuts. Had it ever occurred to her to just run away when she saw them? Of, course not. This was Annabelle I was talking about. *Follow them?!* I scoffed. How had this woman survived this long?

"And they caught me."

I stopped walking, my eyes widening at her revelation. I immediately began scanning her for injuries, but she looked the same as always. *"Are you okay?"* I signed.

Holding her arms out, she smiled. "Jane, I'm fine. Promise. They were totally cool. They took me to their place. It's huge, Jane!" She said excitedly. "It's like a little town or something. They built a big wall around an apartment complex. It's a really neat setup."

None of what she'd said so far lessened my anxiety. In fact, it only caused my heart to pound even harder. She hadn't just found a few people. She'd found a huge *group* of them.

"They asked me questions, but I promise, I didn't tell them where we were. They were cool. They gave me the ham and said they'd like to start trading with us. See? Perfect set up. We could help each other."

My heart rate slowed, but I still wasn't convinced that this group was as perfect as she'd claimed.

"I showed a couple of people how to shoot." She held up her bow. "Easy."

I let out the breath I was holding. *"This is too dangerous. What if they hurt you?"*

Even if it was possible Annabelle understood that lengthy sign, she didn't see my question, too busy staring at the fence.

Her face pinched in confusion. "Huh. I could have sworn the fence was bent right here."

I looked up and down the fence line but didn't see anything other than a few places where the plastic inserts had cracked or chipped off. Nothing of concern there. *"Wrong place?"* I signed.

She shook her head. "No, look." Bending down she gripped the chain link at the bottom and gave the fence a little shake. It didn't move.

Crouching next to her, I peered at the spot she was pointing at. You could definitely see where the metal had been bent - it still curved slightly in - but it had put pushed back in place and one zip tie held two links together at the very bottom. From the look of it, the hole wouldn't have been big enough for a person to get through. That wasn't what had both Annabelle and me looking at each other, a hint of fear in both our eyes.

"Who fixed our fence?" Annabelle asked the question I had been thinking.

Angry barks and growls erupted from somewhere in the distance causing us both to jump to our feet.

Poco!

2

HIS FULL ATTENTION WAS ON THE FENCE WHEN WE found him. The fur on his back stuck straight up and slobber flew from his mouth as he barked incessantly. Not getting too close to the aggravated animal, I did my best to soundlessly step up to the fence. Annabelle stood on the other side of Poco, her bow and arrow ready as she looked for the trespasser. It was obvious, though, that whoever Poco had found wasn't on this side of the fence.

My grip tightened around the handle of the knife I held at my side as I slowly leaned forward to look through one of the broken plastic slats. The same scene from this side greeted me. Acres of trees stretched out farther than the eye could see. Brown leaves littered the ground, dark from recent rain. Not seeing anything of interest, I leaned back and went to another opening to peer through. Again, nothing.

Something cold and wet landed on my nose and I rubbed it away before taking another look through the fence. The wind picked up and carried a few leaves, but other than that, there was no movement.

The fence shook slightly and I jumped back with a gasp as Poco's barking increased. My gaze automatically went to the top of the fence, but what I saw was not what I'd expected. A fat squirrel had landed on the fence and walked it like a tightrope as Poco followed along, growling as if the squirrel had made some grave offense.

"Damn it, Poco!" Annabelle groaned as she lowered her bow. "A squirrel? Really?"

Sighing, my shoulder loosened, but I didn't put up the knife. The adrenaline was too fresh for me to totally relax. Maybe Poco hadn't been barking at a trespasser, but someone had messed with our fence.

"Maybe, I'm wrong," Annabelle shook her head as she swung her bow back over her shoulder. "Maybe we missed the fixed hole when we walked the fence."

I shook my head no. It may have seemed like something easily missed for some people. But not for me. I had been meticulous in my search for any and all breaches.

Annabelle sighed. "I'm heading back to the house. I'm exhausted."

I nodded for her to go. After two days of hunting for supplies and having to watch her own back, she needed to take a day to rest. Taking one last look around, I slid my knife back in the holder at my ankle and signed, *"Rest."*

I hadn't forgotten what we'd been talking about before and I would definitely bring it up again later. Maybe my expression gave me away because Annabelle rolled her eyes at me.

"You're such a worrywart. It was fine. I know it's hard for you to believe, but they were *nice.*"

Without responding, I turned away from her.

"You're going to walk the fence line again, aren't you?"

I waved her away as I got to work. Raindrops continued to fall sporadically causing me to pick up my steps, but that didn't mean I wasn't thorough. I looked over every inch of the fence, stopping a few times to look through the small holes the cracked plastic inserts made. The closest thing I'd seen of interest was a flesh eater stumbling around too close to the fence for comfort. However, taking him out would be more work than worth it. He couldn't climb the fence. Hell, he probably didn't even know it was a fence.

My steps were almost silent as I walked away to finish my inspection. Poco trotted by once or twice before running off toward the house. The poor pup probably couldn't decide who to stay with and protect. Me or his mommy.

Annabelle. I rolled my eyes thinking about the crazy woman. A group? She'd found a group. Of course, she had. And they're *nice*, she'd said. I wondered how true that was. Could there really be more people out there? Decent people? I just wasn't convinced. In my mind, Kaden, Mason, and Annabelle were exceptions. I'd been damn lucky to run into them.

The rain picked up and I quickened my steps as I thought about luck. Was I lucky? Mason was dead. And Kaden had never come. My mind took me back to those days with them. To the long hikes and even longer one-sided conversations Mason would have. I grinned thinking about him even as my eyes began to sting. I blinked, killing the tears before they could fall. I hadn't allowed a single one to slip since the day I'd left. I didn't know why. Only that allowing myself to cry would be surrendering. But surrendering to what, I wasn't sure.

By the time I finished checking the fence, I was soaked from head to toe. The air had gotten much colder and the clouds had darkened to nearly black. I'd been wrong about the weather. I'd been expecting light snowfall, not a thunderstorm.

A sudden gust of wind pushed me back and I ducked my head as I ran for the house. Just as I reached the clearing a streak of lightning blinded me, seconds before thunder boomed, shaking the ground beneath my feet. I blinked to clear my vision, blindly reaching for the door then hurrying inside.

As I peeled off my wet coat, Annabelle ran into the kitchen, her face pinched with worry. "Did you see, Poco?"

I shook my head. Last I'd seen him he was running toward home. Outside, the sound changed and I peeked out, my brows furrowed when I realized it was now sleeting. Thunder shook the house and I shivered. It looked bad out there.

"Shit. I think something happened to him."

I caught sight of her panicked face and sighed. She was right. Poco was a smart dog. He wouldn't still be out there if something hadn't gone wrong.

Reaching for my coat, I shivered as I slid my arms through the icy fabric. It held no more warmth and weighed a ton, but it would be the only thing protecting me from the stinging ice and rain as it pelted me from all sides.

"What are you doing?" Annabelle asked.

Clamping my teeth together so they wouldn't chatter, I

finished the last button and signed with shaky hands, *"Out."*

"No," she shook her head. "He'll be back soon." Though her tone was unconvincing.

I would have gone anyway if her eyes hadn't widened with fright. *What?* I mouthed.

Grabbing my shoulders, she pulled me further into the kitchen and began yanking at my coat. "You can't stop shaking."

I slapped at her hands, but her glare stopped me. Annabelle rarely became angry.

"Damn it, Jane, your lips are turning blue."

Once my coat was gone, she pointed a finger at me, demanding I stay before rushing out of the room. By then the shaking had turned violent, and I decided it might be a good idea to listen to her. When Annabelle returned, I was still standing in the same spot, my arms crossed over my chest as I did my best to hold in as much body heat as possible.

She helped me take off my wet clothes, then wrapped me in the towel she'd brought before pushing me toward the living room.

"I already have a fire started. Go lie down on the couch." Bending down, she plucked my clothes off the floor. "Here," she handed me my knife. "I'm going to hang these in the mudroom to dry."

With my hands full with the towel and the knife, I couldn't sign, so instead, I mouthed one word, *"Poco."*

"He'll be fine," she said, her green eyes darting away. "I'll call out for him. He's probably having the time of his life out there, running around in the rain."

Except it was sleet, not rain.

Hoping she was right, but knowing she wasn't, I laid

down on the couch and pulled the thick wool blanket off the back with a sigh. Already, I was warming. I stared at the flickering flames in the fireplace, my eyelids drooping as I listened to Annabelle rummage around, making little noises here and there. I liked the sound. Which surprised me. I remembered it had been not too long ago I wanted nothing more than to be alone.

Just as I was drifting off, I heard Annabelle calling out for Poco. I tried to open my eyes, to get up and go help her, but exhaustion won. My last conscious thought was for our four-legged friend. I hoped he was okay.

3

AT FIRST, I THOUGHT IT WAS THE LAUGHTER THAT HAD woken me up. But the sound wasn't familiar and who would be laughing? Maybe it was just a remnant from a dream. I was still tired, and my body wanted nothing more than to go back to sleep. Eyelids fluttering, I was seconds away from heeding the call to do just that when Annabelle let out a shriek followed by a yip from Poco.

Eyes now wide open, I jolted into a sitting position and turned toward the noise coming from the kitchen. Another voice followed the scream. This one deeper, more like a rumble, but too soft for me to understand. My mind sped to find a solution, but only one conclusion could be made. I had to help Annabelle.

My feet found the floor soundlessly, my fingers already gripping the knife as I shifted to get off the couch. With my other hand, I caught and held the towel close to my chest and rushed to save my friend. Turning the corner, my brain was only seconds ahead of my actions, which meant when I threw the knife, the man sitting at our kitchen table was lucky I'd shifted my arm an inch to the right.

"Jane!" Annabelle gasped, jumping off the floor where she and Poco were playing tug of war with a piece of rope. But the man I'd almost killed didn't utter a sound. He stared wordlessly at me, his expression not even registering surprise. Neither did mine as I took stock of our visitor.

My eyes raked over him, taking in everything they could. The shadowy kitchen obscured his eyes, but if I had to guess, I would have said they were a murky brown. Wild, dark hair fell in loose curls to his shoulders. Wet, it was slicked back on top of his head from pushing it off his face. A face half covered in a full beard the same color as his hair. If I had to guess, I'd say he was in his late twenties, early thirties at most. But that would be stretching it.

My gaze caught on a Ying Yang pendant attached to a small brown feather that hung from a leather cord around his neck. The pendant looked old and cheaply made, and the paint on one-half of the pendant had peeled off. The feather was real from what I could tell, but I didn't know bird biology well enough to say what kind.

As far as the rest of him… His white long sleeved cotton shirt and light blue jeans were both damp. Meaning it was pretty clear how physically fit the guy was. *He won't be easy to take down.*

Out of the corner of my eyes, I could see pieces of clothing hung over the kitchen chairs. There also a black backpack on the floor next to his naked feet. But instead of checking these items over, I kept eye contact with the stranger. I had no weapon now. No clothes either. Just the towel. He had to know the tables had turned in his favor. I knew it. Which is why I couldn't look away in case he decided to attack.

Without breaking eye contact, he reached behind him and with a jerk, pulled the knife from the wall. He flipped the blade smoothly in one hand and I pressed my lips together to stem my jolt of surprise.

The corner of his eyes creased with the clench of my jaw and my own eyes narrowed.

Flipping the knife once more, his fingers gripped the blade as he held it out to me. When I made no move to take it, he raised a single eyebrow, as if to say, *I dare you*. I don't know why, but taking the knife would feel like defeat.

Annabelle sighed heavily. "This is stupid," she remarked just before she stepped between me and our guest, effectively ending our stare down. "Here." She handed me the knife with a glare, then sat down in the chair across from the man who's gaze now rested on her instead.

Crossing her arms, Annabelle huffed. "Jane, you should apologize."

Both my brows shot up. I'd expected her to spout excuses for allowing a stranger into our home. Or maybe thank me for trying to defend her, necessary or not. Or at the very least, tell me to calm down. Because that's how Annabelle was. But, this? Me? Apologize?

"He saved Poco and you almost killed him," she accused.

I flicked a glance to the man and saw skepticism written all over his face. My shoulder pulled back. Did he really not know how close he'd come to dying?

"Aidan, don't give me that look," my friend said, causing me to give her a suspicious look of my own. *Does she know this guy?*

"You came this close," she pinched her thumb and forefinger together. "I've seen her throw. Jane never misses."

Aidan's gaze rested on mine once again and this time it held a measure of respect.

His chin dipped once. "Then I owe you my thanks."

I shrugged.

"Jane."

Teeth clenched, I blew a breath out through my nose then nodded. It was the best I could do without my hands.

Noticing this, Annabelle said, "Oh, right. Why don't you get dressed? When you get back, we can talk more."

Talk? Was a miracle about to take place? Would I be cured? She couldn't hear my sarcasm and my arched eyebrow was ignored, of course.

Not happy, but knowing I had no other choice, I gave our visitor, Aidan, one last warning glare before heading upstairs. Dog savior or not, I was not happy with him being here. If I had any say in it, he wouldn't be here for long.

4

WHEN I'D BEEN SIX YEARS OLD, I'D TRIED TO RUN AWAY from home. I'd found a book bag in my father's closet one day while playing between schoolwork. Sliding it over my shoulders, I'd strutted up and down the hall, pretending I was going to a real school just like normal kids.

As I pretended to wave at a nonexistent friend, loneliness had crashed upon me. Back then, there weren't many meet-and-greets or group events for homeschooled children. Especially for kids like me. The *special* one*s*, as my mother would call me. Her favorite photograph was a picture of a red rose amidst a bouquet of black and white flowers. She would point at the only colorful flower and say, "That's you, Jane. My special flower. My special girl." At six years old, I was already tired of that word. *Special.* I didn't want to be special. I wanted to be one of the black and white flowers. Not the sad, lonely red one. And my youthful imagination had found the perfect solution. I needed to run away and find a new school.

Ready for an adventure and excited to meet new friends, I'd forgotten about my parents and marched, chin up, right to the front door. I only made it two houses down the street before my dad caught up to me.

He walked with me for a while before he finally asked where I was going. *"School,"* I'd signed.

"You go to school at home, Jane," he had reminded me.

Frowning, I shook my head. *"I want to go to a regular school."*

He sighed. "Jane, honey, you know you're special." And that had been the end of it. He'd taken me home, delivering me to my teary-eyed mother who took turns hugging and chastising me for scaring her. At the time, I'd thought that was it. I'd never get another chance at being normal. Until just before dinner, when my dad leaned down and whispered in my ear, "Don't worry, Pumpkin. I'll talk to your mother about school."

I'd been so surprised, so excited that I'd jumped into his arms and hugged him as tight as my little arms could. Laughing, he'd caught me. "No promises, though, Jane. We have to do what's best for you. Our special little girl."

Somehow, I'd known then that I wouldn't be attending a regular school. But my dad had listened to me, and that had been more than enough at the time. Two years later my father was electrocuted while working as a lineman and more than anything I wished I could thank him. My mom had listened to me, but never in the same way he had. I had no doubts in my mind or heart that she'd loved me. But her love made her overprotective to the point of being stifling. And after my father's death, it had only gotten worse.

Now, I walked down the stairs to greet our guest properly, with clothes on and without a weapon. Scratch that, without a weapon in my hand. I'd heard Annabelle apologizing for me as I'd gotten dressed. And I wondered if my distrust of people stemmed from my childhood instead of our current circumstances. Did I not know how to make friends because I'd never had friends? Annabelle was my friend, I argued with myself. But Annabelle had also been the one to take charge of that situation. I'd done nothing, too stunned by her open nature to discourage her. Annabelle had been a unique case. And I didn't think I would be lucky enough to gain a friend the same way ever again.

I hesitated outside of the kitchen entryway. Was I already contemplating a friendship with Aidan? I didn't even know the man. He could be a murderer or a rapist. Maybe he wanted our land, our home. Maybe he wanted my friend. The wall that had been crumbling from the moment Anabelle chastised me for almost killing our guest, sealed back up. That woman messed with my head, encouraging me to trust when I shouldn't. It was going to get us both killed one day.

Shoulders back and chin up, I marched into the kitchen. Aidan sat in the same seat as before, his eyes on my friend who now stood at the stove cooking more canned ham. I narrowed my eyes at the way he stared at her ass swaying to whatever music she heard playing in her head. Feeling my death glare, the man peeled his eyes off Annabelle's ass and met my stare, pink slowly flushing his cheeks. Surprisingly, the sight caused my shoulders to ease, and I raised my brows at him before focusing on the whimpering dog at my feet.

I rubbed the top of Poco's head, paying particular attention to his favorite spot behind his ear. His tongue flopped out and he closed his eyes in complete doggie bliss. I smiled at the sight but it faltered quickly when I realized we had almost lost him. And I owed his savior an apology and my thanks for that reason alone. However, in order to do either of those things, I'd have to reveal my disability. I liked to hide that part of myself until I trusted a person. Again, Anabelle being the exception.

"You look better," Annabelle said to me over her shoulder, her smile tight as she glanced between me and Aidan.

"Let's start over." She sighed. "Jane, this is Aidan," she introduced as if the earlier incident had never taken place. "He brought Poco home while you were sleeping and I told him he could stay here."

When my eyes widened in alarm, Aidan jumped in. "Until the storm passes," he assured me.

A glance out the window showed the storm was already blowing over. The kitchen had lightened up enough that there was no need for candles.

Noticing what I had, Aidan stood. "In fact, I should be going."

Good. He needs to go.

"No," Annabelle rushed to put a plate of ham in from of him, causing me to frown. "Eat first. Then we can talk about it. It's too cold to be out there. And wet. Do you even have a warm place to stay?"

She fussed with his plate, setting the silverware down perfectly. When she stepped back, she pulled at the hem of her shirt. She was fidgeting. My eyes narrowed. Annabelle was nervous. Why? I looked at Aidan. He gazed at his feet, his brows furrowed.

"I should go," he said again.

"You saved my dog. The least you can do is eat some of our food." Annabelle's teasing tone fell flat, but her words sent a ripple of guilt through me. Damn it.

My sigh had them both looking in my direction which caused heat to spread up my neck. *"She's right. Please, stay and eat. It's the least we can offer you,"* I signed.

Forehead creased, Aidan shook his head. "She's deaf?"

Rolling my eyes, I look to Annabelle for help. She giggled. "No. Mute. She can hear you just fine."

"Oh. Sorry.","

"I'm sorry I tried to kill you," I signed to him. *"Thank you for bringing our friend home,"* I gestured to Poco, who had crawled under the table to nap.

Aidan glanced at the dog and shrugged. "I'm sorry, but I don't know sign language."

"Hopefully, she apologized for almost killing you." Annabelle's smile widened along with Aidan's dark eyes. "Oh, and she said you could stay as long as you want."

My eyes narrowed at my friend. That was not what I'd said. One look at my reaction had Aidan's lips twitching. Jerk.

"Did she?" he asked.

Annabelle nodded vigorously, but our guest left his gaze on mine. After a moment, I finally gave him a single nod. Though I'd gritted my teeth as I done so.

"Okay," he said simply and sat down to eat the ham.

Pulling out a chair, I sat down next to Annabelle and across from our guest. He may be coming off as a nice guy, but I would still keep an eye on him.

"While you were sleeping, Jane, Aidan told me Poco had found him and wouldn't leave until he followed him to the house." She reached down to pet the dog under the table. "Wasn't that so sweet of him? Poco was trying to help Aidan get out of the cold. But if Aidan hadn't come, Poco could have gotten hurt out there. They saved each other," she sighed.

I just barely stopped myself from rolling my eyes. What in the hell was wrong with my friend? I'd never seen her so moony-eyed. Then again, I hadn't known her that long. Maybe she was always like this with the opposite sex.

"Did you fix our fence?" I asked.

He looked to Annabelle, who translated for me, before answering. "Yeah. I found a couple of spots. I think a wild animal was trying to get under the fence and made a mess."

"That was nice of you!" Annabelle beamed.

"I'm sorry about being on the property," Aidan said to me. "Your barn was the only shelter I could find."

"Do you stay in the barn regularly?" Annabelle asked.

Aidan shook his head. "Not anymore."

When he didn't elaborate, Annabelle asked, "You were living here?"

His dark brows furrowed as he looked down at his now empty place. "No," was all he said before sliding his chair back. Both Annabelle and I watched silently as he began gathering his things.

When he slung his pack over his shoulder, Annabelle leaped to her feet. "You don't have to go, yet. It's still cold out there. And your clothes are wet."

Anabelle may have been the one who had spoken, but when Aidan looked up, it was my gaze his connected with. I stared back, my expression mirroring my thoughts. Indifference. Though it might sound cold, I didn't care either way if he stayed or not. He was a grown man and could make his own decisions

Aidan turned away, dropping his gaze before it collided with Annabelle. "Thank you for your hospitality," he said, then slipped out the back door.

"You're welcome," Annabelle replied, but he was

already gone. Her brows lowered as she stared at the closed door. Then she turned to me, her lips twisting into a scowl. "Well, that was rude," she huffed.

I nodded, agreeing with her assessment. He was rude. Though I hadn't really thought so. But weren't friends supposed to support each other by male bashing from time to time?

Annabelle scoffed. "Not *him*. You!"

My neck jerked back at the daggers being thrown from my friend's eyes. Her face had turned red, and I swear steam blew out from her nostrils. Though, to be honest, it could just as well have been the cold causing her breath to fog instead of what I imagined was her blood boiling.

"He helped Poco. You should have been nicer," she accused. "And what was with the knife? You could have seriously hurt him."

When I couldn't come up with an answer, I shrugged. Which must not have been appropriate, because her expression only darkened.

"You know, Jane, not everyone is out to kill you. They're too busy running from people like you."

The words hit me like a punch to the stomach. Standing up from my chair, I signed slowly, *"What?"*

Throwing her hands up, Annabelle sighed as she shook her head. "You figure it out, Jane." With that last parting shot, she stomped out of the room, leaving me feeling like maybe I'd been too quick to call Annabelle a friend. Or maybe, she was right.

5

———

DAYS LATER, AND AIDEN HADN'T SHOWN HIS FACE AGAIN. However, the sneaky man had been doing things around our little farm. After a failed attempt to hook up a generator to the well, we'd left it out on the porch one night only to wake the next morning to running water. How he'd hooked it up while we'd slept, I hadn't a clue. But I had a sneaking suspicion Anabelle knew more than she was letting on. I also notice another spot in the fence that had been fixed with zip ties.

Although I grudgingly appreciated the help he'd given us, and a part of me had this overwhelming urge to trust him, I still held reservations about his motives. What was his purpose? Why was he hanging around?

Setting up another log, I hefted the axe and brought it down as hard as I could. The blade stuck into the top of the wood but didn't split it completely. I was getting better, though. I hit the center that time.

With Annabelle not speaking to me, there was nothing for me to do. I'd walked the fence a dozen times, killed a few flesh eaters that had gotten too close, and now I was chopping wood. Or trying to, at least. After two more tries, I finished off the log and went for another.

I thought about going for another supply run, but that was a waste of energy. Not to mention dangerous. We had enough for keep us fed until our next scheduled run. Though as I swung the axe once more, my shoulders screamed, and a list of other supplies we could stockpile came to mind. Like aspirin, I thought as I rubbed at my sore neck.

The door to the farm house slammed shut, catching my attention. Speaking of sore. There was the other pain in my neck. Though I'd spent my days trying to find things to keep me busy, I thought of nothing but Annabelle's last words to me. They may have been harsh but they also rang true. There was no way I would be able to change overnight. I didn't have it in me to trust easily, but I also understood that if I didn't adjust my attitude then one day I would hurt someone innocent. And that scared me more than anything.

In other words, Annabelle was right. Wasn't that a hard pill to swallow?

Setting down my axe, I met up with my friend as she jogged down the porch steps. Her eyes set on mine for a moment before she brushed past me. Poco had run down the steps behind her but stopped by my leg for a pet before following his master.

I stared at her back as she walked away without a word. She was still pissed. Understandable. But didn't I deserve more than a brush off? I narrowed my eyes at her back. Why did she have her pack and bow and arrows? Was she going somewhere?

Catching up, I tapped her arm to get her attention. Her shoulders stiffened under my touch and she wouldn't look at me, but she did stop walking. Coming around to face her, I stared at her annoyed expression with one of my own.

"Where?"

"Not your business."

Though her clipped words hurt, I didn't show it. *"Not fair."* At her shrug, I sighed. *"I am sorry."*

With her lips pressed tightly together, she stared at me, her moss green gaze filled with a mixture of anger and hurt. The sight caused a pang in my chest and I reached out for her, stepping forward, my arms open. At first, I thought she'd refuse. She had to know how hard this was for me. I wasn't a hugger. But after a torturous few seconds, her lips twitched and she wrapped her arms around me in a tight embrace.

"You're forgiven." She sighed against my shoulder. "I just worry about you. You've closed yourself off so much. It's not good for you."

Her words hit home, but I wasn't ready to deal with them yet. Instead, I stepped back and raised my eyebrows, willing her to admit a different reason for her anger.

Puffing out her cheeks, she blew out a breath and chuckled. "And I *really* liked Aidan," she admitted. "Too bad you scared him off."

He hadn't run too far, I wanted to say. *"Sorry,"* I told her instead.

"No, you're not."

"Yes, I am."

Annabelle shrugged. "It's okay."

I nodded, but I hadn't forgotten my first question. *"Where?"* I asked again.

When she bit her lip, her expression full of guilt, my shoulders stiffened.

"I'm going back to that group."

Her reply sent searing pain through my chest. She would really leave me so easily?

At my wounded look, Annabelle's eyes widened and she reached out to touch my arm. "Just for a day or two. I promised them I would come back to give another archery lesson. They said they'd give us some apples for my time."

"Dangerous," I signed, though I knew nothing I said would stop her.

"Jane, I really want those apples," she pleaded. When her bottom lip popped out, I had to cover my smile with my hand. She was good.

"Come with me!" she said suddenly. "Then you'll see there's nothing to worry about."

I glanced around the small farm. *What about the house? The Land?* We couldn't both leave.

As usual, Annabelle was able to read my mind. "The house will be fine."

I thought about it for maybe a minute, but it was more than just the house that made me hesitate. I wasn't ready to meet these people.

"No," I signed.

"Jane—"

"Not yet."

"Next time?"

I paused. *"Maybe."*

Crossing her arms, Annabelle lifted her chin to glare down at me. "Next time," she demanded.

Not wanting to promise anything, but also willing to keep the peace, I signed, *"We'll see."*

"Good enough." Giving me her signature bright Annabelle smile, she hugged me again and left, leaving me behind to worry. Again. That girl was going to drive me insane.

"I'm taking the van," she called over her shoulder with a wave. "It's less than a day's drive. I'll be back before you know it."

Less than day's drive? That close?

Once Annabelle was out of sight, I turned back around, my eyes drawn to the remnant of my attempt to chop wood. We had a decent size pile of firewood stacked next to the house, but it wouldn't be enough to get through the winter. However, the thought of picking up the axe again caused my shoulders to twinge. I was going to have to be careful and work progressively harder until my body was used to the new abuse.

Deciding I was finished for the time being I went inside to get warm and found plenty to keep me busy. We might be in the middle of an apocalypse, but that didn't mean we had to live in a dirty house.

I began upstairs, but I didn't get much further than putting fresh sheets on the beds. As I smoothed a clean quilt over the top of my mattress my gaze was drawn to the picture frame on the nightstand. It faced away from me, the black cardboard backing mocking me for my cowardice. Averting my eyes, I swallowed hard, flattened another wrinkle with the palm of my hands, and prepared to move on to the next room. But my eyes had other ideas. They strayed towards the framed once more. Unable to completely remove the photograph without guilt pulverizing my stomach, I'd turned the picture around our first night in the house. I didn't like photographs. They were a reminder of all that we—*I*—lost.

The house was full of pictures. They hung on the walls, sat on the mantle, the side tables, and nightstands.

So far, I'd done well to either avert my eyes to the point I didn't think about them anymore, or I would flip them over. At first, Annabelle had tried asking why, but after a while, she stopped.

Now as I leaned over the mattress, my gaze glued to the back of the five-by-seven wooden frame, my heart raced, my palms itching to reach for it. I already knew what I'd see. What I'd been avoiding since moving in.

The floor creaked beneath my feet as I rounded the bed and reached for the frame with shaky hands. Taking a deep breath, I flipped it over then had to sit down when my knees gave out. Dressed in matching black caps and gowns, Mason and Kaden stared back at me, smiling wider than I'd ever witnessed. Even Kaden looked happy, his blue eyes sparkling with an innocence he no longer possessed. His arm was wrapped around his friend's shoulders in a protective gesture that was true to Kaden's nature.

My eyes stung and watered and I almost put the photo down, but I forced myself not to. Annabelle's words swirled around in my head. I *was* closed off. I'd always been a little. I'd had to be. But my time with Kaden and Mason had opened something inside me. Something that I had immediately sealed back up the minute I'd left them in that cabin.

I hadn't yet dealt with Mason's death, hadn't grieved, hadn't cried. He wasn't the only loss I'd tried to bury deep inside. And though I owed it to myself and Annabelle to deal with these issues, I wasn't sure I was ready.

Crack, thump!

The melancholy spell broke and I jumped to my feet. A few seconds passed before I heard it again.

Crack, thump!

I placed the picture frame on the nightstand, again facing away. I probably should have been annoyed by the interruption. But after the heavy emotions I'd just drudged up, I didn't have it in me to be irritated. I was too relieved for that.

A glance out the bedroom window overlooking the back of the house confirmed my suspicions. Hair pulled back in a messy ponytail at the nape of his neck, Aidan swung the axe, hitting his mark perfectly. The log split down the middle with a *crack*, then fell apart, hitting the ground with a *thump*.

My lips pursed, a little peeved at how easy it looked for him. Then I shook it off, deciding to learn instead of glare. He'd taken his coat off, leaving him in a red flannel shirt, the sleeves rolled up to his elbows. It was pretty cold out there, but I could attest to how hot it got while splitting wood. I'd almost thrown off my coat too.

After he placed another log in position, I noted his grip on the axe. While his left hand wrapped around the bottom of the handle, his right was placed just under the blade. He swung and when the axe cut through the log effortlessly, his left hand was now placed next to his right at the bottom of the handle. Watching the whole process again, showed me he was sliding his hand down mid swing.

Although the lesson had been interesting, I couldn't stand there all day. Sighing, I stepped away from the window and left the room. There was still dust bunnies to eliminate, and as much as I would love to ignore Aidan, I was trying to take to Annabelle's advice. She hadn't come out and said I needed to be nicer, but it had been implied.

At the bottom of the stairs, I pulled on my boots and coat, preparing myself for the cold. But before I stepped outside, I remembered to retrieve one of those miniature spiral notebooks and a pencil.

"I didn't think anyone was home," Aidan said as he leaned the axe against the pile of logs still waiting to be split.

When he turned back around, I raised an eyebrow then quickly wrote, "*So, you wouldn't have come if you'd known I was here?*"

"Smart," he murmured, referring to the notebook. "I'm not sure it would have been a good idea," he answered me.

I wanted to ask him why he thought that, but I had an idea. I had tried to kill him last time.

"*Are you living here, now?*"

My mocking glare softened when a red blush spread up his neck. "No. I mean…"

"*It's okay,*" I hurriedly wrote.

"It is?"

"*As long as you keep fixing things,*" I teased.

His snort made me smile, and I realized I'd gotten comfortable with Aidan pretty quickly. The unusual sensation caused me to tense, ruining the happy and relaxed atmosphere.

"*Thanks for all your help,*" I wrote. "*Especially with the generator. But if you hurt Annabelle, I will kill you,*" I warned.

His eyes met mine and what I saw there surprised me. Respect.

"Understood," he agreed. Then his eyebrows slanted into a deep v as he glanced around the property. "Speaking of… Where is Annabelle? I saw her leave with the dog. I had assumed you'd gone with her."

Gripping the pencil, I scribbled the answer. Aidan's

face darkened as he read, and when he finished, his eyes flashed at mine. "She went alone? Where is this group?"

His reaction surprised and pleased me. My gaze wandered over his features for the first time without suspicion. I still didn't know Aidan enough to fully trust him, but his obvious worry over my friend went a long way in my book.

"Not sure. But she did say it was about a day's drive from here," I wrote.

If Aidan's expression could become any darker, it did. His brown eyes looked almost black, and a vein throbbed in the side of his neck as his jaw clenched.

He gave me a single nod. "I think I know which group." He picked up his coat and a backpack that had been sitting nearby and swung it over his shoulders as he walked passed me without another word.

I turned to watch as he walked toward the tree line for a moment before it finally hit me what he was doing. Jogging to catch up, I tapped him on the shoulder. He turned around with a questioning lift of his brows.

"Why are you going after her?" I wrote.

When he didn't answer, I continued with, *"She told me it was safe. They are a good people."*

He snorted. "No one is *good* anymore."

"Annabelle is," I wrote down.

His gaze stayed on the paper much longer than necessary before he nodded slowly. "I think I know which group she's dealing with. And I don't trust them."

Turning the page on my notebook, I wrote, *"I'm coming with you."*

When I looked up he was already nodding, a light smile lifting his dry lips. "I'll wait while you grab your stuff."

I ran back to the house, checking over my shoulder to make sure he did what he'd said. I was surprised to see him right behind me as if he hadn't hesitated to follow. I made note of it in my head, adding it to the surprisingly long list of Aidan pros I'd gathered.

6

TO TELL YOU THE TRUTH I'D BEEN A LITTLE SURPRISED to see Aidan's motorcycle, but I hadn't been unhappy about the discovery either. I might be overly cautious when it came to people, but riding a dangerous vehicle was a dream of mine, so I'd thrown on the helmet he'd handed me and climb on eagerly, my grin widening when I saw his answering smile.

To my delight, he'd driven with speed. Probably faster than was safe. Stopping for quick breaks to stretch and drink water every hour or so. We made it to our destination just before sundown and I tried not to be disappointed. I wanted to get there as quick as possible. For Annabelle's sake. But I'd had so much fun. I hadn't felt so free is a long time.

We'd hidden the bike and as we walked the last mile Aidan talked. What he told me about these people caused my stomach to tighten with worry over my friend. He admitted that no one had harmed him. In fact, he'd never witnessed them physically harm anyone. However, they had a tendency to recruit new members with a tenacity that bordered on harassment.

I thought he might be overreacting. But he'd shaken his head and said, "You'll see." Those words alone caused my anxiety to heighten. Especially as we neared the entrance to what looked like a well-protected military base.

They'd used the sides of those metal shipping containers as a wall surrounding the complex, which had been a smart move, though I did wonder exactly how they were able to get them there. Especially because of the location. Although off a side street and hidden by a good number of trees and foliage, the complex was still close enough to the main highway and the town limits where the flesh eaters were numerous. Aidan and I had done a lot of maneuvering to get around them.

"I'm not sure if you want to keep your," Aidan waved his hand around his throat, "a secret or not, but I'll tell you right now, it'll be hard. The leader likes to talk. Also, don't promise them anything. They take those seriously."

I'd barely been able to nod before a man appeared above one of the sections of metal wall in front of us. His blonde hair had been cut close to his oval shaped head and was so white he immediately reminded me of the tip of a cotton swab. His green military fatigues were exactly what I expected, however unpredictably, he pointed no gun at us. In fact, from what I could see, he held no gun at all. Only a two-way radio in his right hand.

"Aidan!" he called. "It's good to see you back." His wide, fake smile had my eyes slanted toward my companion. Aidan's shoulders were stiff and something throbbed just below his jawline, but he lifted his chin. "Ames," he greeted.

"Let me just call this in and I'll open the gate." Lifting the two-way, his gaze landed on me. "Who's your companion?" he asked.

"Jane," Aidan answered. "She's a friend. Her roommate," he stumbled over the word roommate, "is here doing a trade. She wanted to join her."

"Name?" Ames clipped.

"Annabelle."

Ames' face softened. "Oh? You're Annie's friend?"

I stiffened at the use of the nickname and saw in my peripheral Aidan do the same, but I nodded my answer all the same.

This time Ames' smile held a leer I didn't like. "Annabelle is a special girl."

The silence between the three of us after that statement was full of so much tension it became hard to breathe. Or maybe that was my rising anger that had me holding my breath.

"Yes, well, Jane would like to speak to her," Aidan finally growled. I could tell he was holding himself in check. Why? I wasn't sure, but I could also see Ames knew it too and was delighted by Aidan's reaction. He winked at me, his smile widening with my scowl.

"Hey, boss," Ames said into the two-way, "Aidan's here with a friend of Annabelle's. They want to talk with her."

The radio crackled then a male voice replied, "Oh, how nice. Let them in. I'm on my way to greet them."

"All right. You heard the man. Come on in." Ames disappeared from the behind the metal wall and I looked to Aidan.

"Follow my lead," he whispered just before the two connecting metal walls in front of us began to part. It was then I noticed the trench dug beneath the two walls and as we crossed over the line, I could see wheels had been attached to the bottoms. Smart, I thought again. Then all thought ceased because we were inside and it was nothing like I expected.

7

THE TWO-LANE ROAD CONTINUED INTO THE COMPLEX and lead toward two tall buildings. But first were the gardens. I could see cornstalks, and leafless trees, but other than that the dirt rows were empty. It was easy to see the state was only because of the winter and not the maintenance. The rows were neat and without weeds and I could even see a few people in the far fields doing something. I had to squint to see them, that was how far the grounds reached. At least the length of a football field on each side. Maybe two. They would take a lot of work to keep up. I wondered how many people lived there and what they did with all of that food.

"I'm so glad to have you back, Aidan." The middle-eastern accented voice interrupted my scrutiny and caused my stomach to tighten in a weird way. Weird because I didn't know why.

I turned to face the new person and my brows furrowed. He was a couple of inches shorter than Aidan, with short curly brown hair highlight with gray at the temples. His jaw, covered in a day or two's worth of growth, was the same color as his thick, dark eyebrows and accented his bladed nose and brown eyes. I didn't recognize him at all, but the more he spoke the queasier I became.

"How have you been? Are you in need of anything?" he asked Aidan, his smile wide and welcoming.

"No. I don't need anything." He paused before adding as an afterthought, "But, thank you."

"Ames tells me you're looking for the lovely Annabelle. Is that correct?" The man's heavy gaze landing on me for the first time. "You must be the friend she speaks so highly about. Jane? Yes? I'm Naahir."

"We would like to speak to Annabelle." I was thankful for Aidan's interruption and nodded my agreement.

Naahir gave us a tight smile but lifted his palm with a wave. "Then, by all means, follow me. She's in the field teaching a few of us how to shoot the arrows. Talented girl," he remarked. "She'd be an asset here." He looked over his shoulder and smiled at me. "We would be honored to have both of you stay."

I kept my face blank and he eventually turned back around.

"I'll give you a quick tour as we walk and you can think about it."

Aidan and I exchanged a look. Was he just being nice, or was this the beginning of the endless recruitment tactics?

As we neared the apartments, my breath caught in my throat. There were people walking everywhere. Living people. A woman carrying a baby on her hip smiled as she walked past me, but all I could do was gape back at her.

"Here is the housing section," he said, gesturing wide.

There were two rows of brand new looking apartment

buildings, eight altogether, four on each side, with a courtyard in the center. Each concrete building was five apartments wide and six tall.

Naahir pointed to a tunnel that led beneath one of the buildings, "Garage-parking," he said. "Also there's a swimming pool, water slides, tennis court, fitness center, sauna, Turkish bath, a pergola in the garden, a children's playground, plenty of security, and a very large generator. We also have solar power."

He turned to smile at us. "Many of those things are not necessary or are just plain useless now. But I was very lucky that all of this was mine. This complex was days away from the grand opening when things went badly." Sadness laced his voice.

"This area is not known for its luxurious living, but there had been interest. People wanted quiet, privacy, and beautiful views," he said, waving at the mountains visible in the distance.

Aidan snorted softly beside me, but either Naahir didn't hear him, or he had ignored my companion.

"I'd hoped to own the most lavish apartments in the area," Naahir continued. "And I succeeded, however a little too late. But it must have been fate because now look at us. We are a thriving community of over a hundred, with extravagances that many in this world are having to do without."

My eyelids felt permanently glued to my brows. I couldn't stop staring at everything. It was amazing. There were people hanging out on their balconies, and the smell of cooked meat wafted past my nose. Someone was grilling. The awe on my face couldn't be concealed. This place was like looking back in time.

Though the sun was still visible just above the horizon,

it would be getting dark soon, but the darkness wouldn't be an issue here. Lights had already started flickering on inside the apartments. Electricity! I made a mental note to talk to Annabelle about this. Maybe we could figure out how to generate solar energy.

Aidan nudged my shoulder and I turned my wide eyes to him. He nodded his head at something behind me. My gaze followed then narrowed on the soldier standing next to our tour guide, his posture indicating he was there to protect him, and my wonderment dimmed.

I saw the whole place in a different light now. While entranced by the living quarters I'd completely missed a number of men wearing military fatigues. I counted eight as they strolled around the grounds, blending in with the people as they talked and laughed together. Some nodded to the soldiers, but most acted as though they didn't even see them. And unlike Ames at the gate, a few had visible weapons on them.

"Impressive, isn't it?"

Our tour guide stared at me expectantly, so I gave him a nod. It was indeed impressive. My gaze collided with the soldiers standing next to us and a tingle prickled the back of my neck. Impressive as it was, though, something felt off.

A few minutes later we were past the living quarters and heading toward another long stretch of land. There were men playing a game of touch football, and a small distance away from them was a group of people lined up in front of makeshift targets. I could see Annabelle walking from person to person, showing them how to hold their bows. But what held my focus was beyond them.

About fifty yards away, a truck had parked just inside

the walls of the complex, it's bed full of lumber. Four men unloaded the long treated planks of wood, one by one.

I slowly came to stop, my gaze unmoving from two of the men. After setting down a piece of lumber, they strolled back to the truck, their light-hearted laughter causing me to flinch.

"Ah, we are getting ready to build a guard tower for the east gate," our tour guide stopped to explain, but as he continued to detail his plans, I ignored him in favor of the scene before me.

One of the men turned his face in my direction, confirming my suspicions. It was a dream come true. Or maybe my worst fear realized. In that moment, it was a little bit of both. Because one of the men I couldn't stop staring at was Mason. *My* Mason. Only he wasn't dead and he wasn't a flesh eater. And the guy he was currently laughing with was his best friend, Kaden. The same man who said he would come find me, but never had. The man I'd been waiting more than two months for.

At some point, someone had flagged down Annabelle. But when she came to stand next to me, I was frozen in place, unsure how long I'd been there.

"Hey, guys. What are you doing here?" Her finger came into focus as she pointed to where I was looking. "Aren't those your guys, Jane? I didn't know they were here."

No. They weren't my guys. Not anymore.

Sensing our stare, both men turned as one to look my way, and my pulse leaped. I wasn't ready. So, I did the only thing I could. I turned on my heels and ran. Right into the solid brick wall of Aidan's chest.

8

_____

A WAR BROKE OUT INSIDE ME, AND I GRITTED MY TEETH as the battle began. My muscles clenched with a need to run toward the men, while my brain urged me to run in the opposite direction. Anger, confusion, and relief fought for the top emotion. My skin itched and burned and I wanted to crawl right out of it. Finally, I held my breath and waited. Waited for my heartbeat to slow and those emotions to burn themselves out. Until suddenly, I was just numb.

"Is she all right?" I heard someone ask. "Jane? Miss… I'm sorry, I forgot to get your last name," Naahir was speaking, but I was too busy learning how to breathe again to acknowledge him.

Naahir… Naahir… The familiar name suddenly clicked. He was the one inside the cabin the day I'd left the guys.

Aidan's fingers tightened on my shoulders. "Are you all right, Jane?" he asked softly.

I turned to where Annabelle hovered next to me and

caught sight of Kaden and Mason. They'd gone back to work as if they hadn't seen us.

"I need to go. Leave. Go. Now," I signed erratically.

"She's deaf?" I ignored Naahir, my focus completely on getting out of there.

"Okay. All right," Annabelle mumbled as she watched closely. Her wary eyes darted to where Kaden and Mason were, then back to me. She nodded then turned quickly to Naahir. "Thanks for the apples, but we need to go. Come on, Poco."

I hadn't even noticed the dog until then. He stood from where he was leaning against Anabelle's leg, his back rigid as though he'd heard the seriousness of her voice.

Though his gaze narrowed in confusion, Naahir wasn't able to get out a reply before Annabelle dragged me away, with Aidan and Poco following.

"Wait," he called. "You just arrived. Besides, it's almost dark. Maybe you should stay here until at least first light."

"No need," Annabelle said over her shoulder, her stride not breaking as she turned down his offer. "My headlights work just fine."

———

The drive back to the house was long and silent. I rode shotgun with Annabelle while Aidan followed behind on his bike. Poco slept in the back seat as usual. After announcing she was there to listen if I wanted to talk about it—or sign about it, she'd joked—she fell silent and hadn't said a word since. That was hours ago. I hadn't been much of a conversation starter either. I'd spent the time staring out the window. It was pitch black and only the lights from the van cutting through that darkness allowed you to see the road. A light snow had started falling a couple of hours ago. It was the only view keeping me entertained. Which wasn't much.

Not being able to take the silence any longer, I turned to Annabelle but hesitated. She was sitting forward a bit in her seat, her eyes glued to the road. I wanted to smirk at my daredevil friend who I now knew was a safe night driver, but my frustration over my disability caused my fingers to fist in my lap instead. I glanced out the window and sighed.

"Is the silence getting to you too?"

I gave my friend a grateful smile and nodded. She glanced at me quickly with a small smile of her own before looking straight again.

"I'm sorry. Driving at night makes me nervous. And with the snow, I'm a little— Shit!"

The van swerved, clipping the flesh eater that had walked in front of the van. The tires went off the road, sending me slamming into the passenger side door before Annabelle righted the vehicle. Gripping the 'oh-shit' handle, I turned to look behind us.

"Aidan!" Annabelle slowed but didn't stop as we watched the headlight behind us.

When the motorcycle stayed steady, we both let out a sigh of relief, but it was short lived. As soon as the first thump, thump sounded, Anabelle cursed and pulled over onto the side of the road.

Aidan came to a stop behind the van and hopped off to get a closer look. The front passenger side tire was ripped to shreds. "Must have run over something when you swerved to miss that flesh eater back there."

I gave the area a cursory glance. The night was quiet, except for the hushed sound of snow fall. But it wouldn't stay that way long. It never did. Not wanting to continue being sitting ducks, I signed, asking Annabelle for the spare, but Aidan beat her to it, grabbing the jack and a wrench from the back too. Then proceeded to take over.

I could have argued, but there really wasn't a point. If he wanted to change the tire, then fine. The quicker we got out of there the better. Standing back, I let Aidan do his thing while I kept an eye out. I was worried about that flesh eater we'd hit. Would he follow the sound of our vehicles? We hadn't driven very far before pulling over. He was slow, but he could catch up quickly.

It wasn't long before I heard the sound of something dragging against the pavement. At first, I'd thought it might be Aidan, but I walked away from them, far enough to hear something that had my eyes widening.

Whipping my knife out from my boot, I walked briskly to the flesh eater heading this way and took him out before running back to the van. Annabelle was kneeling next to Aidan, not paying enough attention. When I grabbed her shoulder, she gave a shout that had my hand covering her mouth.

Lowering my hand, I began signing and her eyes widened before translating to Aidan, who had stopped working on the tire to watch me.

"Listen," Anabelle told him.

A car was coming.

"Can you finish the tire?" Annabelle looked between the road and the old tire still attached to the van, her expression a mixture of worry and hope. I could have told her it was no use. No way could he get the new tire on and secure in time.

Aidan confirmed this with a shake of his head. "No. We have to hide."

When Annabelle opened the side of the van, Poco jumped out, immediately growling at the trees, looking for the threat.

"Go with Aidan. I'll stay with Poco and put on the tire."

Before I could finish signing, Anabelle was shaking her head, no. "You know that was too much for me to understand, but I'm a hundred percent positive you're telling me to leave. I'm not going without you."

I didn't have time to argue. Headlights appeared in the distance. And they were moving fast. A flesh eater suddenly stumbled out of the trees causing Poco to go crazy. Aidan looked at the flesh eater and the approaching vehicle, then met my eyes. He needed to get Anabelle out of here. It wasn't about leaving me behind; it was about the odds. Could all three of us survive the threat? Not likely. But if he took Anabelle, two of us would.

I gave Aidan a subtle nod, and he pulled a struggling Annabelle toward his motorcycle. "We have to, Annabelle," he told her softly. "She has a better chance hiding if we lead them away."

"But if we stay, we can fight them off," she pleaded.

Ignoring her argument, I waved her on before rolling under the van. Seconds later the bike roared past. I clutched my knife in my hand as the sound of its engine disappeared, replaced by the roaring of another getting closer.

I heard Poco in distance, growling at what I assumed was another flesh eater. I wasn't too worried for him. He was fast and would run if he needed to.

I gripped the handle of my knife in one hand, my nails

dug into the asphalt with the other, and I held my breath as a trucked came to a stop next to the van. I cursed under my breath. I'd hoped they would have followed Aidan. He could have lost them easily.

The door opened, but the engine didn't cut off. This gave me hope.

"Jane?"

The sound of my name caused me to jump. The movement must have been enough to gain the attention of a flesh eater I hadn't realized was so close. He reached for my foot from the other side of the van.

"Jane, come on!"

Without thought, I rolled out from under the van, away from the grasping fingers of the flesh eater and whistled for Poco. He leaped into the back of the truck without hesitation. Mason slid into the cab after me just as Kaden hit the gas, causing the tires to spin out before eventually we lurched forward and sped away.

At first, the only sound inside the dark cab was my heavy breathing. My eyes were glued to Kaden's white knuckled grip on the steering wheel.

It started with my hands. They trembled in my lap, and as I stared down at them it hit me all at once. I faced Mason. He was looking back at me, his brown eyes full of concern. The same brown eyes I'd thought I would only ever see again in my nightmares. The ones I'd thought had turned dull and dead...

"Shhh."

The whispered hush brought me out of the dark where I realized I was straddling Mason's lap. My hands were gripping his shoulders, my face pressed against his neck as my tears soaked the collar of his shirt. I sobbed, though silently, my chest hiccupping as I tried to catch my breath. I'd thought Mason was dead. I'd thought he was gone forever. But he wasn't. He was here. Alive. My shaky fingers dug into his shoulders to be sure and though he grunted, he didn't pry them away. Instead, his arms tightened around me, pulling me as close to him as possible.

The entire drive was like that—me wrapped around Mason—my tears coming and going. Then the truck came to a stop and I heard the whine of the window being rolled down and softly spoken words. The truck rolled forward then came to another stop before Kaden cut the engine.

I slowly released Mason and slid off him to stare through the front windshield out of hot, swollen eyes. We were home. Anabelle stood with her hands on her hips next to the house, her lips pressed together as she watched us. Aidan spoke to her and though her chin lifted, she slowly lowered her hands and turned to go inside. The truck rocked as Poco jumped from the back to follow them.

"Are you okay?" Mason asked.

Was I okay? I shook my head. No, I wasn't okay.

"We should talk," Kaden, the ever practical, stated.

Instead of replying, I signed for them to come inside. Getting the hint that I wasn't ready to talk, Mason finally opened the door.

"Are you okay?" Aidan asked as we entered the living room.

I waved away his question and looked for Annabelle.

He pointed down the main hallway. "She's washing the blood off of Poco."

"Who are you?" The clipped question came from

Kaden. He and Mason stood in the center of the room. Kaden's arms were crossed over his chest, his brows pulled down tight. Mason, on the other hand, looked as laid back as I remembered. His hands hung loosely at his sides, the corners of his mouth were tipped up just slightly. It was his wary gaze that made me realized he didn't feel as easy going as he played.

Aidan mimicked Kaden's posture, crossing his own arms and staring him down. "Who are you?"

Kaden's jaw ticked and the tension in the room constricted the air in my lungs. Not in the mood for a pissing contest, I stood next to Aidan and faced the guys. Kaden only blinked, but Mason flinched as if I'd done something hurtful. I had no idea what, though.

"My friend."

After reading my hands, Kaden's gaze landed hard on mine, full of accusation. Again, I didn't understand. And truthfully, I was too tired to care.

"What did you say?" Aidan's softly spoken words had me facing him, but it was Annabelle who answered.

"You're our friend." As she came to stand on the other side of Aidan, she smiled at him. "I told you so."

"And you? Who are you?" Mason asked.

Annabelle's smile never wavered. "I'm Annabelle Price. Good to meet you. I've wanted to kick you guys in the balls. Especially you." She turned her sickly-sweet smile on Kaden and this time he flinched. "My girl, here, deserves better."

My lips parted on a silent gasp. I hadn't told her much about my time with Mason and Kaden. She knew about Mason's bite, but I never even spoke about waiting for Kaden.

Her soft brown eyes met mine and her smile wavered.

"I know you, Jane." Then her attention split between Kaden and Mason. "I know you saw her today. I watched you look right at her. Why did you pretend you hadn't? But then come after her? What's your deal?"

I looked at the floor because I'd wondered the same thing. I just hadn't been brave enough to ask.

"We've kept Jane's existence a secret from Naahir," Kaden replied willingly, then turned his burning gaze on me. I couldn't look at him. Not yet.

"Before we admitted to him that we'd lied, I thought we should talk to you first," Mason said softly.

The silence stretched between us, to the point of awkwardness, until Annabelle stepped in, saving me.

"You guys can stay here for the night. It is your house, right?" she asked Mason. He swallowed then gave her a single nod but said nothing else. "But I expect you won't be staying long?"

Aidan and I shared a look. With her stiff posture and pursed lips, Annabelle no longer looked like our usually sociable friend.

Needing to escape the tension, I excused myself.

"Get some rest, Jane. I'll show the guys to a room. Oh," she turned to Aidan, "And don't think for a minute I'm letting you sleep outside again."

Shaking my head, I climbed the stairs, my muscles screaming with each step. It had to be three, maybe four, in the morning. And it had been a long day. I was wiped.

Kaden followed me to the bottom of the stairs. "Jane, we should talk. There are things that need to be said."

I shook my head again, not even looking back while he'd spoken. Instead, I thought about the tasks I needed to perform before bed. First on the list was I needed to be clean. My teeth were grimy and my clothes stunk. Thinking about anything more was just impossible. He and Mason would still be there in the morning. I paused mid-step. Or would they? I lowered my head and continued up the stairs. I would find out soon enough.

9

I STARED IN THE MIRROR AT MY REFLECTION. THE flame from the single candle didn't give me much light but it was enough to showcase the dark circles under my eyes and small lines around my mouth. Frown lines, my mother had called them. Did the lines mean I frowned too much? I emptied my face of all expression. It didn't make much difference. I still looked tired. And sad, I realized. I looked really sad.

Closing my eyes, I took a cleansing breath, thinking it wasn't very cleansing. At least my outside felt clean. I looked down at my night shirt. It wasn't really mine. I'd borrowed it out of Mason's bag back when we were still on the road together. At the time, I'd thought I would have plenty of opportunities to return it. Then afterwards, it became a security blanket of sorts. My brows furrowed. I should give it back to him.

Then my shoulders slumped. What was that other thing my mom used to say? When life hands you lemons, you make lemonade? Well, what if life takes away all the lemons? What do you do then?

When I looked back up, it wasn't just my reflection staring back at me in the mirror. Another face appeared. One of two that haunted my dreams on a regular basis.

Turning around, I lifted my chin to meet Kaden's stare. A stare I couldn't interpret. If memory served, not being able to read his face was customary. He had never let me in. Never would. I'd thought differently at one time, but I saw it for what it was now. Lust, loneliness, need. Those are as viable reasons to connect with someone as love. Nothing wrong with that. As long as you realize it, know it, own it, and act accordingly. And act I would.

My anger and confusion gave way to relief. They were both alive and well. I couldn't ask for much more than that. But I would ask for more. Just one more thing. Knowing our time was short, I'd made the decision to sleep with them. I was lucky Kaden had come to the door before I'd lost my nerve.

I palmed the condoms I'd brought with me into the bathroom. I'd had them stashed in my room for when Kaden came back. It was fortunate I hadn't thrown them away when it became obvious he wasn't coming.

He's here now. A little voice reminded me. The voice was right. He was here. *For now.*

"Jane, you need to know that I planned on coming to you. I…We had to take care of some things…"

Kaden's words trailed off when I took my first step towards him. Watchful, his gaze fell to the hand I placed on his bare chest. He'd come to me without a shirt, wearing only a pair of thin basketball shorts. Maybe he'd only been getting ready for bed. Or maybe he'd known what would happen between us.

He backed up as I pressed him into the hallway, the

entire time my gaze traveled over him, binding this new memory to my mind.

"Jane…"

My other hand skimmed up his chest, stopping over his heart to feel it beating wildly beneath my palm. Desire did that. So would fear. My eyes lowered to the front of his shorts. Desire, then.

He felt warm and familiar, and I wanted to wrap myself around him, bury my face in his neck and stay there forever. I wanted his hands on me. I wanted his lips on mine. But from the way he was looking at me—like he was fighting the pull between us—it would have to be me who made the moves. Me who touched him. My lips on his.

He swallowed hard as I ran my fingers down his arm before grasping his hand and tugging him into his room and to his bed. A fire was already roaring, chasing away the chill. The upstairs fireplaces were just another benefit to this house. A house that wasn't really mine. I had no hope that Kaden and Mason would stay. In fact, I expected they were only here to apologize for leaving me hanging and would leave at first light. But would Mason want Anabelle, Aidan, and I to stay indefinitely?

I pushed the worry away for now. With only a couple of hours left until dawn, there were other things I needed first.

Kaden sat on the bed willingly, his gaze trained on me. The light from the fire caused his eyes to shine in the dark. His pupils were dilated so wide they hid the beautiful blue I remembered. His hair, now longer than I remember, fell across his forehead. I swept the strands back just as a shadow fell over the doorway letting me know we were no longer alone. Just as I'd planned. Or hoped for anyway.

"My shirt looks better on you than it did me." Mason's low tone held a hint of amusement.

"Jane…" Kaden again, trying in vain to protest.

I could tell what he was doing. He thought I needed to hear his excuses, his reasons for not coming for me. But I didn't need them. I knew it had something to do with the miracle of Mason being alive. I also understood now what they were to me. What I was to them.

I shrugged lightly and threw the condoms on the bed next to Kaden, which effectively shut him up. Then, gripping the hem of Mason's shirt, I pulled it up and over my head, sighing as the cotton brushed against my naked skin. My only covering, my long hair free from its rubber band, slid against my back, causing me to shiver.

Both stilled, their gazes heated and their lips parted with soft exhales.

"God, Jane. You're beautiful." Mason took a tentative step into the room and when I didn't protest, he strengthened his stride to come stand next to me. He trailed his fingers down one of my arms. So sensitive to his touch, I shivered and arched as my nipples beaded in response.

Kaden spread his knees willingly when I stepped into them and his lips softened when I pressed mine against them. Gripping his shoulders, I put everything into the kiss that I was feeling. I nipped his bottom lip, then kiss him hard, shoving my tongue against his. Taking him. Owning him. Because he was mine. They both were. If only for the next few hours while the three of them combatted the loneliness the world offered.

After that, there were no more words, all protests died and were forgotten. Desires and pent up needs took over. Both men stripped off the rest of their clothes and we fell to the bed in a tangle of arms and legs. In some of my wildest dreams, I'd fantasized about being with both of them at once. I speculated what it would be like to lay between them. I'd often wondered if it would be awkward. If one or the other would become jealous or uncomfortable. But none of those things happened.

Kaden's hands slid over my skin, leaving goosebumps in their wake. His lips trailed down my throat, over my collarbone, up my chin, and over my lips. He kissed and caressed me everywhere he could touch.

All the while Mason did so similarly at my back. His lips brushed over my skin, his teeth nipping at my shoulders. One hand buried in my hair, the other grasping my hip, both grips punishing as he thrust into me from behind.

My body was alive for the first time since I'd left them in that cabin all those weeks before. But it was more than that. I wasn't just alive, I was a live wire, in a continued state of arousal, where one orgasm led into another.

Later, when Kaden filled me, he urged the flames to blaze once again. I met his requests with desires of my own. With cravings that needed satisfying. I wasn't just hungry, I was starved.

Sex could be enthusiastic, even passionate. But this was different. This was decadent, carnal. They didn't just fuck me. They worshipped me.

When we finally slowed and our limbs tired, we laid wrapped together, our hearts pounding and our sighs heavy. Replete and utterly exhausted, I was also overwhelmed by how amazing we'd fit together. Though I knew it would only haunt my dreams, I closed my eyes and forced myself to commit each kiss, each touch, each whisper to memory. It would be all I had going forward.

10

I WAS A CHICKEN-SHIT. NOTHING BUT A COWARD. I knew it, but it hadn't stopped me from running.

Waking first, I'd allowed myself a brief and last moment of pure bliss in the men's arms. Then I'd forced myself out of bed and had watched them sleep, waiting for one of them to wake up while preparing myself for their goodbyes. But my courage had lasted a mere fifteen minutes before I'd convinced myself it was best if we didn't do the whole goodbye thing again.

I hadn't just left them with nothing, though. A note lay on the nightstand with my own goodbye. I'd offered them my understanding and wished them luck.

It was for the best. It really was. Maybe it had been a little spiteful, but I'd even closed it with that line.

It's for the best
– Jane

Stuffing my gloved hands into the pockets of my wool coat, I hunched my shoulders and continued walking the fence line. I'd already walked the entire property line twice, swinging by the house once to see both Aidan's bike and Kaden and Mason's truck gone. I was postponing the evitable. An empty house. Or worse, an inquisitive Annabelle. I hadn't seen her when I'd left the house, but she no doubt had plenty of questions. Ones either I didn't know the answer to or were too painful to think about.

The weather and an empty water bottle decided my fate. January could be a harsh month in this altitude. The snow the night before covered the thick piles of leaves beneath the trees. Closer to the house, in the clearing, there was an inch or two piled up. My lungs burned from the cold and my throat had turned dry.

As appealing as thirsting to death sounded in the moment, I chose to head indoors. But when I saw who sat on the porch steps waiting for me, I decided living was overrated. Turning and running away was my second choice. Unfortunately, he saw me coming before my body could cooperate.

Mason stood as I approached. He stuffed his hands into his coat pockets and waited, his eyes boring into mine. When I finally stood in front of him, my heart felt like it was beating in my throat. The gaze he held me with wasn't lively or bright. They weren't the eyes I'd come to know. Instead, they were dull. Not lifeless, but devoid of the happiness I'd always associated with Mason. It reminded me of my own eyes. The ones I'd stared at the night before in the mirror. Sad. He was sad.

There were about four steps between us and my fingers twitched in my pockets wanting to close the distance. Instead, I pulled back my shoulders and waited for his sentencing. I could tell by the pinch of his lips that he had something to say. Maybe once he got whatever it was off his chest he would leave for good. The thought hurt, but I deserved it.

"You surprised me, Jane." He titled his head and looked at me even harder if that was possible. "I don't know why. I should have expected it. It's what you do best. Run."

I bit the inside of my cheek, the pain welcoming. I'd been right. He was there to condemn me.

"You can't run from everything. Eventually, there's nowhere to go."

I heard his words, understood them, and even agreed with him. Running was all I'd known how to do for so long that it was still my first reaction. To run and hide meant safety. But we'd been separated for a while now and I'd been doing better.

"I am different."

Mason shook his head from side to side. "I don't know what you're saying." His eyes shifted to the side and he swallowed before looked at me with a new determined expression. "I know you've spent your life listening to everyone. You're probably tired of it by now. But give me a few more minutes. Let me talk while you listen. Then if you want to pull out a notebook or whatever you can."

A perfect comeback came to mind. One where I would mention how much he liked to talk. But not only would he not understand, he didn't look like he was in the joking mood. So instead, I followed him silently into the house.

While Mason divested himself of his outerwear, I heated up some water in a pot hanging over the fire in the fireplace. While doing that, I took off my own coat, hat, and gloves then made us each a mug of coffee using the hot water and the French press Annabelle had found.

Mason hummed with his first sip. If I could, I would have done the same. The hot, bitter liquid warmed my insides going down. I didn't always drink my coffee black, but finding creamer now was impossible. I suddenly imagined an irritated Annabelle milking a cow so we could make flavored creamers.

"What are you smiling about?"

I looked up from my coffee to see Mason watching me. My lips tilted down and I shrugged. It wasn't important.

"Last night was…" Mason paused. "Last night was great. I don't regret it, but I do wish the three of us had talked beforehand."

I looked around the room and listened for signs that anyone else was there, essentially Kaden, then recalled both vehicles were missing.

"Where is—" I stopped when I remembered Mason didn't know what I was asking. I rubbed at my forehead with one hand and sighed. This is why being alone worked best for me. I frustrated myself a lot less when alone.

Mason's eyes followed my gaze around the room. "Oh. They all went to get the van. Kaden and the dog, too. Just in case."

I raised an eyebrow, surprised he'd known what I was asking, but he ignored my questioning look and ran a hand through his messy hair. I watched his fingers work through the knots, surprised to see how long it had gotten. His beard had also grown out. I'd noticed it the night before as it scratched against my sensitive flesh. Kaden's too. I could still feel the effects on the skin around my neck, breasts, and between my thighs. I shivered at the thought. Just another memory to hold on to.

"I don't know where to start." Mason wouldn't make eye contact with me. Instead, he stared down into his mug. "I'm immune to their bite. The flesh eaters. No one knows how I survived. But I did. And to test it, I was bitten again."

I sucked in a startled breath and held it.

He finally looked up then. "As you can see, I'm okay. I didn't even get sick the second time around."

My breath left my lungs in a whoosh and the momentary fear I'd felt vanished replaced with deep anger. Kaden let this happen? He allowed Mason to be bitten again? What had he been thinking? What had they both been thinking? If I could have talked I would have been screaming.

Mason held up his hands, palms up, his eyes pleading. "I'm fine, Jane. We had to know."

He reached out slowly and placed his hand on top of one of my balled-up fists. He rubbed at it, loosening my grip until he could link our fingers together. The movement calmed me somewhat, but I still had a bone to pick with Kaden.

I watched his face carefully, but it gave away nothing. His gaze was on our linked hands. His thumb rubbed circles on the center of my palm. Tingles shot up my arm, but I ignored them. Something wasn't right about his story. The excuse had been weak. And the more I thought about it, the more irritated I became.

I tightened my grip on his hand, stopping the incessant circling of his thumb. His gaze jumped to mine and there I found proof of deceit in the form of guilt. I ripped my hand away from his.

Standing, he circled the table where I sat and crouch down next to my chair. I went to turn away from him, but the soft pleading in his words stopped me.

"I'm sorry. We should have come before now, but we couldn't."

"*Why?*" I mouthed. Nothing about the story he told me should have kept them away. He could have at least come to let me know he was alive. Instead, he'd left me here thinking he was dead. I pushed back the stinging tears and gritted my teeth.

On an exhale, his forehead met mine. I closed my eyes and sighed along with him. As angry as I was, I couldn't push him away. He smelled like the almond soap in my bathroom and beneath that it was just him. I never could describe the scent. He smelled like Mason.

"It wasn't safe. I had to make sure I was well. If I'd gotten you sick…"

I opened my eyes to find his staring straight into mine. They were glassy with unshed tears.

"I wouldn't have been able to live with myself, Jane. I…" He swallowed, choking on his words. It was too much. His words were thick with emotion and my chest ached.

"I'm sorry—"

I brought our lips together in a crushing kiss. I twisting in the chair to grab his shoulders, my fingers digging into the hard muscle as pulled him closer. He moaned into my mouth and kissed me back without hesitation before his hands circled my waist and lifted me easily out of the chair and onto the table.

My legs wrapped around his waist as he stepped between them. His mouth never left mine the entire time. His tongue stroked and tasted, fanning the flames that had begun inside of me. He pulled on my braided hair, tilting my head back sharply so his mouth could devour mine. My belly burned, my core ached, and I ground myself against him, begging him to ease my suffering.

With a curse, he ripped his lips away from me and if I could I would have whimpered. Mason's ragged breath told me, he wasn't too happy with the separation either. I leaned forward to capture his lips once again but he stopped me.

He cursed under his breath. "This wasn't my plan," he panted. "I promised myself I wouldn't do this."

His grip on my hair slackened, then fell away.

"You don't want me?" I signed the words, forgetting he couldn't read them.

"Are you kidding, Jane? I want you more than I want to breathe right now." His hands flexed on my waist as if to bring home his point.

His eyes, dark with desire for me stared hungrily into mine before he leaned slowly toward me. The feel of his palms sliding up my ribcage and the warm breath blowing gently across my face distracted me for a moment and I almost succumbed. Almost.

My hands came up between us, pushing his upper body away from me. He leaned back, keeping my pelvis tight against his, distracting me further when the bulge in his jean pushed firmly against me.

Taking a shaky breath for control, I signed, *"You understood?"*

I wasn't expecting Mason's cheeks to flame, but that's exactly what happened.

He ducked his head and grinned sheepishly. "Sorry. Yeah, I understood you. I... well, Kaden has been helping me learn. I'm not fluent by any means, but I'm getting there."

In such a short amount of time? The average person could take years to attain a beginner to intermediate skill level. The man must be a genius. Though, I was just as surprised at how fast Annabelle was learning.

Maybe I should have been upset by his devious attempt to get me to listen. But I wasn't. I was oddly pleased. He'd take the time to learn my language. That meant he'd been planning to come for me.

I trapped his face in the palms of my hands and brought his parted lips to mine, kissing him softly, with tentative nibbles. It didn't take long for my hands to slide down his chest and wrap around his back. He pulled me close, pressing into me, and I let go. I kissed him with fervor, giving him everything I had, telling him without words what the last few months had done to me.

Unable to wait for him to take it further, I shifted on the table and reached between us to unbuckled his belt. I pushed my hand inside and ran my palm over his black briefs. Groaning, he finally came on board with the plan and helped me by kicking off his shoes and sliding his jeans to the floor.

Once he got his shirt off, he reached for my jeans, yanking them down with vigor. I smiled when they got caught in my boots and he cursed. But once he had them off, he was standing back up, smiling at me too. While he'd been busy with my shoes, I'd taken off my top and bra.

His grin turned wicked at the sight of my naked breasts and thin lace panties. The panties weren't practical, and I didn't wear them often, and I wasn't even sure why I'd worn them that day. Biting my lip, I watched as his finger trailed gently over the front of my panties, thinking maybe I'd known why after all.

Mason's admiration didn't last long. He shucked my panties, flicking them aside before bringing us skin to skin. I shivered as my nipples scraped against the soft hairs on his chest. The desire that ignited in me was visceral and just as forceful as the night before. However, I couldn't help but feel the empty space that should have been Kaden next to us. There was no guilt. But I ached for him as much as I did Mason in that moment.

Slowly, my body fell backwards, meeting the cold wood of the table beneath me. My breath caught in my throat as Mason's smile dropped, and his hooded eyes took in my body, stretched-out and waiting for him. I may have taken charge the night before, but I had a feeling from the firm line of his jaw, he would be the one taking over this time around.

Both wrists in one hand, he pressed them to the table above my head and kissed a hot trail from my forehead to my nose, over my lips, landing on the delicate spot in the center of my throat. I swallowed under his lips and felt him grin. He was driving me mad.

"Jane." He placed a kiss on one side of my collar bone, then the other. "Jane. You're the most beautiful creature on this earth."

He moved lower, his hands caressing my sides and stomach as his breath danced over my skin. My back arched, thrusting my breasts towards him. He teased me with soft kisses until I trembled beneath him. Finally, his mouth came over a nipple at the same time his fingers found the heated juncture between my thighs, circling my throbbing clit. My breath whooshed out of my lungs and I gripped the end of the table above my head, needing something to hold onto.

Mason brought me closer and closer to the edge, easing back, before driving me crazy once more. I was on the precipice for so long, or maybe it had been mere seconds, but it felt like forever before he finally lifted my legs, wrapping them around his waist to sink his cock deep inside me.

Boom! Exploding into a million tiny pieces, I flew to the heavens and beyond. Beneath the sound of the blood roaring in my ears, I heard Mason's soft words. "That's it, Jane. Let go. Let me love you." Then he cursed and pumped his hips harder to combat the tightening of my channel, ending with one last hard thrust punctuated by the hoarse call of my name.

11

We were pressed together so tightly not even air could flow between us. My leg muscles flexed around his hips and his arms contracted at my sides. The house was quiet and all I could hear was the soft huffs of our mingled breaths. It was a wonderfully peaceful moment that lasted not nearly long enough.

We broke apart when the sounds of tires over gravel reached our ears. Our housemates were back.

With a reluctant sigh that I mirrored, Mason pulled away. We needed to hurry if we didn't want to get caught, literally, in our birthday suits. But a soft curse made me hesitate as I reached for my bra.

Mason ran a hand through his hair, then rubbed the back of his neck, clearly upset. "We I forgot protection, Jane. I'm sorry. Shit! I wasn't thinking. I hadn't planned on this…"

I kept my face perfectly blank as Mason continued to needlessly apologize. The blame didn't land solely on his shoulders. Mark one down for another stupid mistake on my part. I'd gotten lucky the last time, with Kaden. Would I be so fortunate twice?

I took a moment to think about the date. If we crossed both fingers and toes, we should be okay. The chance of me getting pregnant was slim and the relief was instantaneous.

"It is okay."

"No, it's not. That was irresponsible of me…"

Hearing a car door slam, I held up a hand. We had no time for this discussion. Mason nodded before quickly shoving his feet into his pants legs. Both in a rush, we didn't have time for talking. But once dressed, we took one look at one another and laughed. Or he laughed, I smiled. From our eschewed, half button clothes, it wouldn't take a genius to figure out what we'd been up to.

"If you want to go clean up, maybe fix your hair, I'll handle this." He gestured to the floor.

I tucked the loose strands of hair that had fallen out of my braid behind my ears, frowning at the mess beneath the table. At some point, we'd knocked over one of the mugs, sending ceramic shards and brown liquid all over the place. I would have argued to help, but the voices outside told me I had mere seconds to decide. Stay or go?

After one last glance at Mason, his back to me as he knelt carefully next to the mess, I fled to the hall bathroom. Just as the door closed behind me, the sound of conversation carried into the house from the front door. The room plunged into darkness. Dark enough that I couldn't see a thing. I'd forgotten there was no window.

My searching hands eventually found one the drawer I was looking for, and I pulled out the flashlight. After turning it on, I set it on the counter to free up my hands.

In the mirror, my shadowed reflection looked back at

me. It felt like déjà vu from the night before. This time there was something different. Though the light was dim, my green eyes held a sparkle I hadn't seen in a long time.

I looked away from my reflection, turned on the faucet and grabbed a towel to clean away the evidence of mine and Mason's slip up. The act was sobering and afterwards, I splashed icy cold water onto my face, shocking some more sense into me. Nothing had changed. Mason hadn't said anything about staying. In fact, I was pretty sure he'd confirmed their departure.

I'd just finished braiding my hair when there was a knock at the door. I'd wondered what had taken Annabelle so long to find me. But when I opened it, it was Kaden standing there.

I backed up as he pushed his way inside, his eyes giving away nothing, as usual. But with the snick of the door at his back, his face softened.

"Are you okay?"

I wasn't sure why I wouldn't be but nodded all the same.

He sighed, his relief evident. Then his face changed, and he no longer looked worried. He looked upset. Not pissed off, necessarily, but he was definitely unhappy.

"You left us."

His statement left me thunderstruck. And for just a millisecond, I thought he'd meant the day I'd left him and Mason at the cabin months before. But that couldn't be right. He'd told me to go.

His gaze wandered over my face, then he shook his head lightly. "You didn't have to run this morning. We wouldn't have left you without talking first."

Though his words made more sense, I had a feeling I'd been right about my first assessment.

"You told me to go," I signed to him.

"No, I didn't. I wanted to talk. Last night—"

I interrupted him. *"Not last night."*

He stared at my hands, his chest rising and falling a little more deeply than when he'd first entered the room. Then his eyes lifted to mine.

"You told me to go," I repeated.

The muscle in his jaw pulsed and his eyes hardened. His signature pissed look.

"I know," he growled. "I know I told you to leave, Jane. But I didn't expect you to do it."

Tears popped into my eyes so quickly, I gasped. I'd always felt guilty for leaving them without a fight. I just hadn't been woman enough to admit it. I'd ran away. I should have stayed. I should have fought. I should have—

Suddenly, I was in Kaden's arms, his big hand pressing my head to his chest.

"I'm sorry, Jane. That wasn't fair. I'm sorry. I'm not angry with you. I'm really not. It's just the whole situation. It's fucked up and I missed you so much."

Kaden's rambling dried my tears quicker than anything else could. Because Kaden, my Kaden, didn't ramble.

Pulling back, I rubbed a finger down the center of his forehead, smoothing out his furrowed brows. Our gazes lock and heat flickered between us. Pulling my hand away, he brought my fingers to his lips, kissing one, then another, his gaze darkening as he tried reading my expression. Seeing no objection, he sucked two of my fingers into his mouth. His hot, wet mouth. I licked my lips, instinctively leaning into him. As his tongue swirled over the tips I was oddly jealous of my own fingers. I wanted that mouth on mine.

Taking both of my hands, he brought them to the small of my back. The move caused my back to arch naturally and my breasts thrust into his chest. I could feel his breath on me and I slanted my mouth, asking... pleading... Then his lips found mine. *Soft. Warm.* He flicked my bottom lip with the tip of his tongue. *Wet.*

My entire body lit up. My heart pounded and my brain completely malfunctioned. It happened every time either of these men touched me. Something I'd thought would never happen again. I'd spent too many nights in bed doing my best not to think of this. Of them. Of their scent, their taste. How had I survived?

Kaden tasted so good. Better than anything I could remember tasting in my past. And damn, he could kiss. His kisses weren't what I'd call tender, but they weren't rough either. They were passionate and intense. It pulsated through my entire body, making me shine from the inside out.

With a twist and groan from him, I suddenly found myself backed against the door, our bodies smashed against one another. My hands were released and I gripped his shirt tightly in my fists while he alternated between cupping my cheek, my ass, and my breasts. He couldn't seem to stop touching me. It was like the night before had never happened. Like it was all new again.

A knock on the door had us freezing. "Jane? We're back. You okay?"

Annabelle.

The moment came to an abrupt end, and we separated. But only slightly. He was breathing hard and hot on my neck, sending shivers down my center.

"Jane?" Annabelle called again.

I slapped the door twice with the flat of my palm. Our signal that I was good and would be out shortly.

When her footsteps faded away, Kaden titled his head to look at me. This time, his expression was an easy one to read. Guilt. Swallowing, I looked down, watching the rise and fall of his chest.

"We have to leave," he said.

I knew it was coming, so I was nodding before he'd even begun. But then he surprised me.

"Come with us."

My gaze jumped to his and this time, his eyes were pleading. *"What about Naahir?"*

"I'll deal with him. Come with us," he repeated.

When I didn't reply right away he asked, "Did Mason explain?"

"Some," I signed.

Kaden took my hands back into his and brought them to his lips, kissing each knuckle on my left hand before moving to the right. The heat between us spiked once more and my lips parted with a sigh.

Once he kissed all ten knuckles, he pulled them away, the reluctance on his face clear as a bell. I felt the same way. I couldn't get enough of his lips on me.

"As much as I want to stay here with you, I can't. Mason needs me. He…" Kaden looked away, his mouth pressed into a firm line.

Sliding one of my hands out from his, I placed it on his cheek and gave him a look I was sure would convey my understanding.

"I don't want him to get in too deep," he told me. "Actually, he's probably so deep he can't see the surface. I can't let him drown. Someone has to be there to make sure they don't use him up until nothing is left. He may be the answer to fixing all of this." He waved a hand in emphasis. "I know he wants to help, but they will take advantage of his big heart if they can. He doesn't believe me, but I know it."

Kaden's speech left me reeling. And not because it was exceptionally long for the man.

"Wait," I signed, stopping him when would have continued. *"What do you mean? Fix what? What is going on?"*

His gaze searched mine. "He didn't tell you."

Though it wasn't a question, I shook my head.

Kaden closed his eyes and sighed. A sigh full of exasperation, frustration, and just plain old tiredness.

"He's cured."

Frustrated, my movements were jerky as I signed, *"Yes, I know that."*

"Naahir's doctor thinks Mason *is* the cure," he stated. "His blood could save us all."

That, I hadn't known.

12

After the shock of Kaden's revelation had settled, I'd agreed to go back with them. Annabelle hadn't been too happy, but after we gave her a brief explanation of the situation with Mason, she finally relented. Though her approval hadn't been necessary, I'd wanted her to understand and support my decisions. She'd made me promise to tell her the whole juicy story without shortcuts when I got back. I had agreed, but only if she gave me her own juicy details with Aidan. Her blush had been epic.

After a nap, Mason, Kaden, and I drove through the night, reaching our destination early the next morning. According to the men, the people there, though enthusiastic about both gaining new residents and Mason's possible healing powers, weren't bad and the guys were sure of my safety. Those had been their exact words. I'd held back an eye roll. Not only was my safety not their responsibility, but they could never guarantee such a thing.

Ames, the same guy who'd guarded the gate the last time I'd been there with Aidan, let us through. I remembered not liking him much. And when he opened his mouth, I recalled why.

"Well, hey there. Jane, right?" He grinned but his expression was far from sunny. More like malevolent amusement.

He glanced at Kaden then Mason before turning back to me with a smirk. "You know a lot of guys, Jane."

Kaden took a step in his direction, but Mason put a hand on his chest to stop him. I, on the other hand, pretended I didn't know his meaning and shrugged. Men like Ames, if you could even call them that, were only interested in getting a rise out of people. I refused to give it to him.

As predicted, when the three of us didn't rise to the bait, his smirk faltered and he frowned.

"Mason! I'd wondered when you'd be back." Naahir strolled up, a big welcoming smile on his face, which parted in surprise when he saw me. "Jane!"

I gave him a single nod of hello.

"How. Are. You?"

He said each word slowly when an expectant look on his face afterward that stupefied me. Until I remembered my last visit. I'd forgotten. He thought I was deaf.

I bumped my shoulder against Mason's just as he opened his mouth to correct him, no doubt. He closed it and turned to give me a questioning look.

"I am well," I signed to Naahir at the same time I mouthed the words.

His smile widened. "Good. Good. How is Annabelle? Will she be joining you? Oh, forgive me, I've spoken too fast."

Just as he'd been about to ask about Annabelle again, this time slower, Kaden stepped forward into my line of sight and began signing to me. I had to hold back a grin when he didn't repeat what Naahir had said.

"Are you pretending to be deaf?" At my nod, he continued. *"I can't wait to be alone with you again. We never finished what we started earlier."*

I had to work not to blush. Keeping a neutral expression, I replied, *"I'm turned on just thinking about the way you kissed me. I want your lips on me again."*

The darkening of his gaze was his only visible reaction. The corner of my lips tugged up and I had to look down to hide the smirk as Kaden answered Naahir's questions for me.

"Annabelle is good, thanks for asking. But she won't be coming today. I'll let her know you asked after her."

"Kaden, you surprise me. I didn't know you knew sign language." Naahir's gazed flashed from Kaden to me.

Kaden signed while Naahir spoke as if relaying what was being said. And again, it took all my strength not to react.

"My lips want to be on you again. On your lips, your neck, your breasts. Especially your breasts."

"My niece was deaf," Kaden answered aloud.

The words brought me back down to earth. He'd never revealed much about his family to me, and I hadn't asked. Hopefully, now that we'd found our way back into one another's lives, we'd have plenty of time for getting to know each other better. I was no longer worried about sharing myself with Mason and Kaden. Not only did I want them to know me. All of me. I wanted to know everything about them. Everything.

I glanced at Mason. He was watching the exchange between Kaden, Naahir, and I with a pleasant, unconcerned smiled that was belied by the slight twitch of his brows. I was pretty sure only I noticed, though.

"Come." Naahir waved for us to follow him. "I'd love to hear how the two of you know Jane while we make our way to the lab. I also wondered if you've thought any more about what we discussed."

We fell in line behind the man in charge, thankfully leaving Ames at the gate.

"I'm sorry Mason, but we need a little more blood. I hope you don't mind," Naahir apologized.

"No, I don't," Mason replied easily. "Take as much as you need. And we're still thinking about your offer."

"No need to sacrifice yourself. Just a vial or two will do."

Naahir chuckled and gave Mason a smile over his shoulder. His eyes connected with mine and I forced my lips to widened into a stupid grin. Kaden hadn't bothered with "interpreting" this time, which gave the illusion that I couldn't hear what was being discussed.

As Naahir led us through the common area between the apartments, I once again became fascinated by the place. Women and men strolled about, some tending smaller versions of the large gardens that surrounded the compound. A few were hanging up wet clothes on a line to dry.

Children ran screaming past me as they chased one another, their laughter causing my scalp to prickle with unease. But there was no need to worry. We were too far from the fences for flesh eaters to hear. Still, I had a hard time wrapping my brain around this way of life. A life that, from the looks of the faces around me, was much different than the one I had experienced. Worry lines didn't mar the adult's faces. Instead, they smiled and laughed just like their children.

"Do they know what's out there?" I couldn't help but ask. How could they just go about life like nothing had changed? Not a single one of them had weapons that I could see.

After Kaden translated, Naahir stopped to look out over the common area, his smile turning proud.

"Yes, Jane. They know exactly what's out there. They've all lost people they loved. But here," he lifted his arms and spread his hands out. "Here, they are safe. And they not only know it, they feel it."

It all sounded so… perfect. Too perfect. Or was it just me again? Was I so far gone, so damaged I couldn't even trust my own eyes?

Naahir directed us to a smaller building that stood between the two apartment complexes. We walked through an empty office area before entering a hallway in the back. A man in military fatigues met us halfway down, falling in line behind the four of us. Mason and Kaden gave the man a small nod as they passed, seeming unconcerned, but I couldn't' shake the sudden bad feeling at his presence.

"You haven't told me how you know Jane," Naahir said, his voice casual.

"We met a long time ago," Mason answered.

When we reached the end of the hallway, we stopped in front of a nondescript white door. Naahir faced us with an expression I couldn't place.

"Did you?" he asked.

It was the hint of mockery in his voice that sent a chill down my spine. Beside me, Kaden stiffened but said nothing. I wanted to look at Mason, but if I did, the game would be up. Instead, though my heart pounded so loud the men should have been able to hear it, I pretended deaf once again.

Smile in place, Naahir opened the door at his back and gestured for us to enter. It was a makeshift lab or doctor's office. A long counter, covered in medical equipment, spread across one wall. And in the far corner was one of those padded vinyl-covered beds.

Hesitantly, I followed Kaden in, my eyes on the new stranger who waited for us. The woman wore a long white lab coat, goggles and a silly smile on her face as her gaze focused solely on Mason.

"Hi, Mason."

I glanced between the two, my eyes narrowing on the woman. She was pretty. Tall, and slim with soft caramel colored skin, straight nose, and big brown eyes behind those ridiculous goggles. She'd pulled her dark, shiny hair into a tight knot at the base of her skull. A skull I wanted to crush. I blinked at the unexpected and violent thoughts. Jealousy was a foreign sensation for me, and I didn't like it.

"How's it going, Kimiko?" Though Mason smiled back, I took immense pleasure when it didn't quite reach his eyes.

Kimiko lowered her lashes as she pointed Mason to a chair and began the process of drawing Mason's blood. My fingers rubbed together at my sides. I itched to grab my knife and test the blade's sharpness.

Naahir shut the door, leaving the other man outside before coming to stand in front of us. His gaze connected with mine, a small smirk briefly playing on his lips. Then he turned his back on us to speak to Kimiko.

"How many vials are you going to draw today?"

To Kaden, I signed, *"For your sake, do not tell him about us."*

His lips pressed together. *"I have to. He knows."*

"You don't know that."

Kaden gave me a reproachful look that had my eyes narrowing, but he didn't reply back.

"Just two." Kimiko finished, placing a piece of gauze in the bend of Mason's arm. "For today."

She gave Mason another too friendly smile that had my back molars grinding together. Then she placed the vials of his blood into a small white machine.

"We're close to figuring out the secret to Mason's miracle." Though she spoke to me, she threw another grin Mason's way. "But as you can see our makeshift lab is a bit small and we don't have as much equipment as I'd like. That's why it's essential for us to get him to Virginia."

Not understanding, I shook my head. *"Virginia?"* I asked.

Kaden was first to speak. "She didn't follow." Then he signed, *"We were going to tell you. I'm sorry, Jane."*

"Tell me what?"

Naahir interrupted, "I need your answer today."

The firm line of Kaden's jaw ticked as he stared down at the floor. Looking at Mason didn't give me any answers either. Indecision had his lips twisting and his brows sliding together. I shook my head, totally lost.

"I'm sorry, Naahir." Mason's sigh was full of regret. "But I just don't have an answer for you right now."

The room grew quiet for several breaths. In that time, my gaze jumped from the rigid Kaden at my side to Mason, who's expression looked pained, then to Kimiko. She was watching all of us carefully, but her stare lingered on me more often than not, her glare one of curiosity mixed with a hint of spite.

But it was Naahir who I watched carefully.

"That's unfortunate."

The agitated tone of his voice contradicted his stoic expression causing me to go on full alert.

To Kimiko, he said, "Doctor Young, would you please give us a moment?"

After another flirtatious smile aimed at Mason, she strolled out the room, the fanning of her coat leaving behind a citrus scent. I frowned. She even smelled pretty.

Once the door shut behind her, Naahir's attention went back to Mason. "I was under the impression you wanted to help."

"I do—"

He cut him off with a calmly raised hand. "I gave you two the benefit of the doubt. But it seems I was wrong."

His gaze held mine for a moment before looking at Kaden.

"You lied to me. I've known about Jane since the beginning."

Kaden didn't move, but I felt the tension gradually intensifying. Sweat beaded on my forehead and back of my neck. From the expressions on the men's faces, this was an unexpected turn of events.

"The beginning?" Mason probed.

"My companions and I saw the three of you enter that cabin. The one we found you in. And a few of my men watched as your friend, here, ran away. I've known from the moment you told me it was just the two of you that you were lying."

"We were only thinking of her safety." The defiant lift of Kaden's chin was met with a glare from Naahir.

"Then I'm sure you will understand that being faced with such a lie put me in a difficult situation, and I had to secure my own safety."

"And what is that supposed to mean?" Mason asked.

He slowly stood from his chair and took two steps in my direction, bringing us shoulder to shoulder.

"It means, if you decide not to cooperate I have to have a strategy in place. One that would guarantee you will do whatever we ask."

Mason let loose a frustrated growl, throwing his hands up in frustration. "I have done *everything* you've asked of me because I wanted to find a cure as much as you do. And I still do. I… We just need a little time."

"Times up," Naahir snapped. "Your selfishness is costing lives. I had a feeling this would happen. I'd hoped you would have forgotten all about your lady friend, but I did plan for all contingencies. I've had Jane under surveillance for a while now, and have methods of making sure you never see her again. We leave in two days. If you refuse, then I will have to take drastic measures."

It suddenly felt like all the air had been sucked out of the room. I gasped, drawing in much-needed oxygen, any and all attempts of pretending to be deaf to his words thrown out the window. Naahir winked, not at all surprised that I knew what he was saying. We'd been duped. All of us.

Kaden took a small step forward, enough to bring him toe to toe with Naahir. His face was red, his expression so hard and fierce even I wanted to back away.

"Who?" he demanded, the vein in his forehead throbbing. "Who is watching her?"

Naahir smiled. "I believe you'll want to take a step

back, soldier. My men are standing outside this room. If you hurt me, they hurt her."

His gaze sought mine and held. "You're a bit of a trouble maker, aren't you? I can see in your eyes that you don't care if you die, but I bet my own life you care very much for Annabelle's. I know you can hear me just fine. Be a dear and tell your men to do as I say."

13

THE THREE OF US WERE TAKEN TO AN APARTMENT AND told that in no uncertain terms were we to leave. If we left before it was time for Mason to go with Doctor Young, then Naahir would give the signal to his watch dog. For Annabelle's sake, we did as we were told.

Hours had passed with none of us able to voice our thoughts. We spent our time in weighty silence. Mason paced the living room, from the front entrance to the large glass windows on the other side. Back and forth, his fingers clenching his hair, then smoothing out the strands. Sometimes he would stop, murmur to himself then shake his head before pacing once more.

Kaden studied each room, examining the ceiling, vents, even checking under the tables. I wasn't sure what he was looking for but it reminded me of those spy movies when the Hero finds the bugs planted in his office. Maybe Kaden thought we were being listened to. I didn't know.

While the two of them kept moving, I, on the other hand, was stationary, standing against the far wall, well away from the windows. I held my knife, blade pointed down at my side, gripping the handle tightly, my finger rubbing at the handle over and over. The feel of the smooth wood gave me comfort as I observed the men.

Kaden stepped out of one of the bedrooms for the fourth time and sighed. "I don't see any devices. But that doesn't mean they're not here."

Taking a deep breath, I slid my knife back into my boot. When I straightened up, both Kaden and Mason were watching me carefully.

"What is in Virginia?" I asked.

My question was for Mason, Kaden placed a finger over his lips then answered using sign language.

"Kimiko worked for the CDC in Atlanta. The place is gone. Wiped out. But there is a lab in Virginia where they secretly stashed back up files, computers, strains of diseases, that sort of thing. She believes it is still up and running and Mason's blood will help them find a cure."

A secret place, I suspected. Operated by the government. They'd always been good at keeping secrets. In fact, I'd often wondered if they'd known about the flesh eaters and whatever caused them before everything went to shit. But that was just a theory. And I'd never been much of a conspiracy theorist.

I began to wonder… If I'd been bitten by a flesh eater and healed, and was told I could help the world, would I? Yes. No doubt in my mind. So, why was Mason hesitating? He'd given them who knew how many samples of his blood and tissue. He'd even subjected himself to a second bite. Yet, he refused to travel to Virginia?

"What are you not telling me?" I demanded.

Kaden shook his head. *"Nothing."*

"Then why not go?"

"We just got you back!" Mason stormed toward me until we were practically nose to nose.

Ignoring Kaden's hush, Mason cupped my chin and pressed his forehead to mine as he spoke. "I'm not ready to let you go again."

Melting, I leaned into him. His words warmed my heart and made me yearn for time alone with him and Kaden. This apartment didn't count. And even if we were completely alone, with no listening devices, I still had Anabelle on my mind.

Giving in for only a second, I placed a soft but quick kiss to Mason's cheek before pulling back and giving him a smile so he'd know how touched I was at his words.

"Annabelle," I signed to him. Then to Kaden, *"Do you think she is safe?"*

His expression darkened. *"Not if she's with Aidan."*

My eyes widened and I practically strangled on my gasp. The indication that Aidan would be the spy was absurd. I shook my head in response. Kaden piercing stare told me he disagreed.

No, I trusted Aidan. I allowed him into our lives. I had let my guard down…

"Who else could it be?" Kaden shrugged.

Unexpectedly, my eyes began to burn as tears threatened to slip down my cheeks. I turned away to gather myself, allowing Mason to offer comfort by rubbing slow circles on my back.

I looked at both men and took a deep breath. *"I have to get to her. I have to leave."*

"We can't leave."

I held up a hand, cutting off Mason's objection. *"I have to go. Not you."*

I had a feeling Naahir didn't care much if I left. As long as Mason stayed behind. That's all he cared about.

Striding to the French doors, I looked out over the balcony. We were on the third floor. Not impossible. But it would be much easier if I could just walk out. I assumed the door had guards, but we hadn't checked.

My steps were light as I hurried to the front door to peek through the peephole. A hand covered mine where it rested on the knob.

"No."

Kaden warm breath tickled my neck and I shivered. Even in the midst of danger, he had that effect on me.

Licking my lips, I turned to face him, to argue, but his mouth stopped me. His lips brushed across mine whisper soft. Just enough to get my heart pounding before he stepped back.

"We will go with you," he signed.

It took me a minute. My brain had to switch focus once again. That tiny kiss had almost wrecked me. I shook my head. These men had way too much power over me. In the past, the thought would send me running. This time, I smiled at the thought. Where Mason and Kaden were concerned, I wanted nothing more than to be wrecked over and over and over again.

"I have to go alone. He will hurt her if you leave," I reminded them.

I could tell from the hard expression on Kaden's face that this could be a battle. A battle I didn't have time for.

Mason stepped forward, his jaw firm. *"No. You will not do this again."*

His hand motions were slow and jerky, but I understood perfectly. Part of me was proud, the other frustrated.

"This is different…" I argued

"Enough."

I froze. Kaden might not have spoken the word, but his burning gaze made feel as if he'd shouted.

"We have to take a chance, Jane," he signed. *"You are not leaving here without us. Not again. Not ever."*

There was nothing to say after that. Mason and Kaden were immovable. And though I worried about what Naahir would do if we were caught before we could get to Annabelle, I was also relieved at having them by my side. I wasn't in this alone anymore. It was a hard concept to accept. But not a hard one to love.

———

No one stood outside the door. In fact, the entire hall was empty, and no one even gave us a second look when we walked slowly out of the building. We found the guys' truck just where we'd left it, next to the front entrance. Ames was there, and immediately, I stiffened. Mason and Kaden, however, acted cool as cucumbers, nodding politely at the guard as we climbed into the truck.

Ames gave us a bored look before opening the gates.

"Does he not know?" I asked.

"Obviously not," Mason whispered under his breath.

I held mine as we drove past. But no one jumped out and yelled, *"Gotcha!"*, and I was able to finally take a deep breath once we were about a mile away.

Again, we drove through the night. And though I was exhausted, I couldn't sleep. A nervous stomach made me nauseous. Our escape had been too easy.

Mason squeezed my knee but kept his attention on the road as he drove. He must have felt the tension in my leg, and I shifted in my seat, hoping to calm down. Kaden sat in the passenger's seat, my hand in his. He faced away from me, his gaze on the passing scenery as his thumb rubbed soft circles the entire drive.

I pulled my hand away to sign, *"Do you really think it could be Aidan?"*

I was having a hard time believing Kaden's accusation. Had Aidan been pretending to… What? Be my friend? Annabelle had been the one to force the issue of friendship. But he had sort of shown up out of the blue. Saving Poco, fixing our fence, hooking up the generators, chopping wood. Had it all been for show?

"I don't know," he said. "It just makes the most sense to me. But you know the guy. We don't. Do you trust him?"

Did I trust Aidan? I thought I had. Now, I was so confused. The more I thought about it, the more I started to wonder. Had I been right about him from the start?

"Distract me," I pleaded with him. I needed to think about something else before I went crazy with worry.

Kaden's brows rose. "How?"

"Talk to me," I signed. *"Tell me about your niece."*

Kaden shifted in his seat and I reached for his hand, bringing to my lap.

"Her name was Caroline," he said, his voice hushed. "And she was the most perfect person I'd ever met."

I looked up at his face to see him smiling sadly, his gaze far away. The sight made me want to jump into his head, experience whatever memory he was seeing. I laid my head on his shoulder and just listened as he spoke, envisioning this perfect little girl I wished I could have met.

"She was seven years old and so smart. Smarter than

me sometimes. Caroline was deaf, but you would have never known she had a disability the way she ran circles around my sister, Kaylee," he chuckled.

"At first, I pitied Kaylee. Caroline's father was a deadbeat who ran off when he found out my sister was pregnant. Kaylee took on the job as a single mom with no complaints, though. Then when we found out Caroline was deaf, I thought it would be too much. But Kaylee surprised me once again. The woman was a machine. Lining up doctors, teachers, making appointments left and right and loving Caroline like an extension of herself. It didn't take long for me realize she didn't deserve my pity or anyone else's. She deserved the world. If only I could have given it to her," he ended on a whisper.

He stopped there and as the silence settled I wanted to ask more. About where he was when the world fell apart. Who he lost. Instead, I signed, *"Tell me about your job."*

His exhale sounded forced. "My job was the reason I lost my sister and her child."

Mason rubbed my thigh lightly. Did he know this story? Was he with Kaden at the time? Or did it happen before the two were able to connect again?

"You were in the military?" I asked Kaden.

"Lieutenant in the Army," he confirmed.

I hesitated, then decided it wouldn't hurt to ask. *"Do you know how this happened?"* I didn't have to elaborate. He would know what *this* meant.

"I…" Kaden hesitated.

"It's okay, man," Mason said without looking away from the road. "It's not your fault."

"No," Kaden agreed. "But it might as well have been." He took a deep breath, then exhaled before he spilled it all. "I don't know what caused the flesh eaters.

There were rumors of a bio weapon gone wrong. But that's not what killed my family. If I hadn't enlisted for a second term... Hell, if I had just gone home as soon as the first report of something crazy happening, I could have saved them." He sighed, tiredly. "I was too late."

He was wrong, it wasn't his fault. But I was sure deep down he knew that. Mason had probably told him a million times himself.

I leaned into him, showing him without words how much I appreciated his openness.

Silence descended upon us, but it was a peaceful quiet. From the slump of our shoulders, I could tell we were all tired, but the closer we got to the house, the more my anxiety increased. By the time we turned into the long winding road that led to the house, I was practically bouncing in my seat. A long litany of threats and curses ran through my head. If Aidan had touched a single hair on Annabelle's head, I was going to kill him. I took that back. I was going to kill him anyway for deceiving us.

It was on the last turn that my worry turned to panic.

The faint morning light caused the flesh eater's eyes to shine eerily in the beam of our headlights. It stumbled across the road, its head turning toward the sound of the truck. But the single flesh eater wasn't a cause for alarm. The open gate to our property and the broken lock dangling off one end was what seized my attention.

"What in the living hell..."

Mason slowed the truck but his surprise only lasted a second before he slammed his foot on the gas and sped up the dirt road to the house, clipping the flesh eater as he passed. As soon as the house came into view, he slammed on the breaks.

All I could do was stare. Flesh eaters were everywhere.

So many I lost count. They walked, stumbled, some even dragging themselves over the ground, their legs missing. It was a herd of them. A big one.

As one, they turned toward us, their teeth snapping as they changed course.

"Holy shit."

The whispered curse came from Mason. Kaden had already jumped out of the truck and was rummaging around in a tool box attached to the bed. When he came back, he had two shot guns and a handgun. I chose the handgun and hopped down from the cab, but before I could run off, Kaden stopped me by wrapping his hand around my upper arm.

Pulling me against him, his rigid body slammed against mine almost as hard as he kissed me. All lips, teeth, and tongue, he kissed the daylights out of me. Then just as quick as the kiss had come, it was over. He pulled out a twelve-inch blade from the holder at his side and ran towards the mob, a weapon in each hand.

"Be careful. I'll keep my eye out for Annabelle." Mason pressed a hard kiss to my forehead then followed his friend.

For a second, but only a second, for I had no more time than that, I closed my eyes and begged the universe to keep my people safe.

Taking a deep breath, I let go of the anxiety, it would only hinder me, and raised my gun. I hit my targets one after the other as I moved forward, taking out the flesh eaters closest to Mason and Kaden, until I ran out of bullets.

Adrenaline pumping, I dropped the empty gun to the ground and slid the knife out of my boot. In a single move, I stood, ramming the knife into the closest flesh eater.

As it fell the ground, I stared into its milky dead eyes and wanted to scream. Whoever had let these bastards into our home would pay.

14

The ground was slick with blood, allowing for an easy home run slide between the legs of the flesh eater. It tripped into the four others that had surrounded me, and I leaped to my feet to plunge the knife into the back of its head. Shoving it forward, the momentum caused two others to fall to the ground. One was trapped by the dead flesh eater, but the other stumbled back to its feet. Meanwhile, I lunged at the two still standing.

Once the small group was taken care of, I turned in a circle looking for more. After what felt like hours of fighting, we'd made a big dent in the mass of walking corpses. However, I still hadn't seen Annabelle nor Aidan.

Sliding my knife out of my recent kill, I looked up, ready for the next when my gaze narrowed on Aidan. Covered in blood and dirt, he swung our axe, chopping off a flesh eater's head. Blood rushed in my ears as I saw red, and without thought, I found myself running full speed in his direction.

He broke away from a flesh eater, just as I was upon him. Lifting his head, his expressions changing drastically in the seconds it took for me to reach him. First relief, then confusion, before dawning realization that it was his blood I was after.

"Wait, Jane!"

Aidan dropped the axe, his hands coming up in a defensive move that I should have paid attention to. But I was too angry. Too scared. Our home had been overrun with flesh eaters and it had been his fault. *His fault!*

Aidan's eyes widened at the exact moment I crashed into him. Though I'd wanted to stab the shit out of him, I'd pulled back at the last minute, not able to cross that line.

We fell to the ground and I immediately brought the knife to his throat, the point grazing the skin just below his beard line. He flinched, his chin lifting away from the blade. I straddled his chest, shoving my knees into his arm pits and brought us face to face.

"Annabelle." I mouthed the word slowly so he'd understand, but it had been a struggle with how tight my jaw was clamped together. I wasn't playing. I wanted to know where she was, and I wanted to know right that second. If he had laid a hand on her…

"Annabelle?"

His chest rose and fell rapidly and he swallowed, his eyes never leaving mine as I gave him a clipped nod.

"She's fine. She's…"

"She's right here," Annabelle said from behind me. "What the fuck is going on, Jane?"

Surprised, I spun around to face my friend and suddenly found myself on my back. Aidan had each of my wrists pinned to the ground before I knew what had happened.

He stared down at me, his face pinched with confusion

and anger. I should have feared him. Instead, I was livid, and I held his glare until he was the one to look away first.

Out of the corner of my eye, I saw Kaden and Mason running toward us, but I wasn't ready to take my eyes off of Aidan. He took a deep breath, sighed, and then without a word leaped off of me to grab the axe. He swung it around, hitting a flesh eater that had stumbled toward us. Annabelle stood next to him, drawing her bow and taking out another.

Getting to my feet, I picked up the knife I'd dropped when Aidan flipped me and tightened my grip on the handle as I continued to watch him under lowered lashes.

Growling, he glared at me from over his shoulder. "We can fight about whatever the fuck this is later. But first, we have bigger problems." With a scream, he swung his axe into another flesh eater.

I had no argument. The immediate threat came first. Once every single flesh eater that had walked onto our property was dead, we'd get to the bottom of how it had happened.

It was a fight, but not a difficult one. Between the five us, we took them out easily enough, and when it was over, we stood in silence as if absorbing the enormity of what we'd just experienced. No one had been hurt, thankfully. However, we were all gulping air, trying to catch our breath and from the looks of their hunched shoulders, they were just as tired as I was.

Mason and Kaden checked the house. The flesh eaters hadn't been able to get inside, and mercifully there'd been no damage. However, there were a whole lot of dead bodies to dispose of.

First, we checked the gate. Someone had used bolt cutters to cut the large iron lock. Opened wide, it had made plenty of room to welcome the flesh eaters. But I had my doubts all of them just happened upon our homestead. Since Annabelle and I first arrived at the small farm a few months before, I'd only spotted a handful at a time. Never in groups this big.

Axe at his side, Aidan studied the property, his brows furrowed. When his gaze met mine, his weary expression hardened and his shoulders pulled back. I caught Kaden's then Mason's eyes. They had the ability to interrogate better than I.

Though his shotgun pointed to the ground, Kaden still looked intimating as hell as he spread his feet shoulder width apart and stared Aidan down.

"Know anything about who did this?"

Aidan didn't reply. Only held Kaden's stare, his chin lifted defiantly.

Annabelle looked back and forth between the two men before setting her bemused gaze on me. "You can't think Aidan had anything to do with this?"

Not waiting for an answer, she stepped forward, putting herself between the men. "Aidan had nothing to do with this."

"You don't know him very well."

Kaden's expression was still hard, but his gaze had softened when he looked at my friend. She, on the other hand, looked like she was ready to spit nails.

"I know him a whole lot better than I know the two of you." Her glare moved from Kaden to Mason. "How do we know it wasn't you who let them in?"

After gaining her attention, I signed, *"I was with them."*

Anabelle's stare went glacial before she turned her back on us to face Aidan. And suddenly I second guessed everything. Because the expression on his face when he looked down at her was so soft, it bordered on awe. He cared about her. What's more, from the way their bodies leaned toward one another, almost subconsciously, his feelings weren't one-sided.

I hadn't been paying attention.

15

THE THICK, COAGULATED BLOOD SMELLED WORSE THAN vomit. And it was everywhere. I held my breath as I peeled the disgusting clothing off my body, throwing them into the farthest corner of the bathroom. They were trash now. There was no point in trying to save them.

Stepping into the shower, I sent a silent thank you to Aidan for his skills at hooking up generators. Though the water pressure was a tad low for my tastes, beggars couldn't be choosers.

Lifting my chin, I sighed as the water cascaded down my head and over my shoulders. I had a lot of making up to do with Aidan. He deserved a fucking gold badge for not only hooking up the water but also the hot water. And what had I done? Repaid his efforts by accusing him of betrayal.

He denied our accusations, then was proved right when we found Poco sitting happily next to a dead body. One that had not been a flesh eater. None of us had recognized the man, but it had been obvious he'd had no business being on our property. A military grade hand-held radio had still been in his hand. We'd plan to talk it over after everyone had gotten cleaned up.

After that, Aidan and Annabelle had walked away without a word to finish removing the dead. We, meaning Kaden, Mason, and I, had followed suit, stacking the bodies at the back of the property where we'd decided to burn them. The only words spoken had been directives related to the clean-up effort.

I'd realized my mistake too late. I had overreacted where Aidan was concerned. I could only hope both Aidan and Annabelle would forgive me eventually.

Shivering at the thought of losing my friend for good, I finished washing and just rested under the warm water. However, as much as I wanted to, I couldn't linger. Someone was most likely waiting for this bathroom.

After drying off, I pulled on a fresh pair of underwear and another one of the guys' t-shirts. I wasn't sure who it belonged too, but it was soft and comfortable and smelled like home.

When I opened the door, Kaden waited on the other side. Though tired, embarrassed, and feeling ashamed of my actions, I couldn't help but give him a small smile.

"Hi."

His return grin barely reached his tired eyes. "Hi." After a short paused, he reached out and brushed his finger over my cheek. "I'm sorry about earlier with Aidan."

I shook my head. *"Not your fault. Mine."*

"I'm the one who put the thought in your head."

Sighing, I placed a light kiss on his cheek, offering him forgiveness. It seemed I could never stay mad at him or Mason for long. They still had so much to explain for, but no matter what, I was on their side. It was a scary feeling.

One I'd been running from. But the running had become more than tedious. I had lived without them for months. And had survived. But it had been scarier and more painful than the feelings I'd been dodging.

Kaden turned his head, capturing my lips with his own. The sweet, absolving kiss turned into a heated full on devouring of my mouth. By the time he was through with me, I was weak at the knees and had to cling to him to find my balance.

Pushing away, I left him to his shower. But at the top of the stairs, I couldn't help but look back. Kaden stood in the doorway, a stupid grin on his face. It was probably the happiest I'd ever seen him. My heart actually fluttered, which I'd thought impossible. But there it was, fluttering like the wings of the butterfly, causing a stupid grin of my own to spread across my face.

Forcing myself to leave before I jumped Kaden in the shower and helped him use up all our hot water, I went to my room, pulling on a pair of sweatpants before heading downstairs. I wanted to find the rest of my people.

I paused.

My people. That had been the second time I'd thought of them that way in a matter of days. Was that what they were? My people?

I visualized each of them in my mind and thought about their strengths and weaknesses. Kaden, fiercely protective over the ones he cared about, made him strong yet weak when it ended up putting him in danger. Mason, who lit up a room with just a smile, was considerate and kindhearted. He wanted to help people. Even those who would no doubt use his generosity for their own gain.

Annabelle, another of my saviors, was not only the bravest person I'd ever known but forgiving and compassionate as well. I worried constantly that her fearlessness would someday get her killed.

And Aidan. I didn't know him that well, yet. But what I'd observed made me think he shared a lot of traits with both Kaden and Annabelle. Not only was he protective, brave, and compassionate, but he balanced out his courage with a healthy dose of caution. The thought made me appreciate him in a way I'd not contemplated before. It also made me even more ashamed of my earlier accusations.

My mind drifted back to the four of them as a whole. They'd each been there for me at one time or another. They were the rocks that had kept me grounded when I would have blown away like the grains of sand in the driest of deserts. Had I ever been that for them? I didn't think so. The thought made me uncomfortable and a little frightened. Why would they stick around someone as undeserving as me? Nonetheless, I was too selfish to let them go willingly.

As I neared the kitchen, I could hear Anabelle and Aidan talking in hushed whispers. For a single moment, doubt trickled in like a slowly dripping faucet, and I thought about eavesdropping. I shut it off quickly before I got myself into more trouble and cautiously entered the kitchen.

Both fresh from their showers, they sat at the kitchen table across from one another, mugs of hot coffee in front of them. They noticed me right away, halting their conversation, though neither looked me in the eye. When I hesitantly sat down, Aidan stood and poured me a cup of coffee. Then without a word, he slid the mug toward me and sat down again, his gaze on the far wall.

I deserved their irritation. And more. So, I took my

penance and sat in silence as we waited for Mason and Kaden to show up, trying to ignore the way Anabelle's leg bounced anxiously in her seat.

When Poco's wet nose brushed against my arm, I obliged him by scratching behind the dog's ears. His tongue lolled out as he panted happily, and I stared into his brown eyes. Red stained his fur in streaks and patches. Though I could tell he'd been wiped down, he would need a bath soon. He was a such a good dog, so ready to help in a fight. If you looked up guard dog in the dictionary, I'd bet there would be a photo of Poco.

His chin rested on my thigh, his eyes looking up at me adoringly. I glanced at Annabelle, then Aidan. Both continued to ignore me, but that was okay. It gave me a chance to study them. Aidan stared down at his coffee, giving clandestine glances at Annabelle. She, on the other hand, wasn't paying attention to him at all. Annabelle gazed out the window, her expression distant, though her leg continued to bounce, causing my attention to land on the two-way radio in her hand.

Annabelle blinked, then looked at me as if she'd felt me watching her. Her unreadable gaze held mine for only a few seconds, then she lowered her lashes, hiding whatever she'd been thinking before looking to the window once again.

When Kaden and Mason finally entered the room after finishing their showers, the tension in the air had become so thick it weighed down on my shoulders. As Mason sat down next to me, Kaden stayed standing, taking in the scene with keen eyes before speaking to Aidan.

"I was the one who brought up your name to Jane. I'm

sorry. But I don't know you, and from the information we had, you were the most logical suspect."

"I get it," Aidan said. "But I had nothing to do with those flesh eaters getting in here. And I definitely didn't open the gate."

I held up a hand. *"I believe you."*

"Of course you do," Annabelle said dryly as she slid the two-way radio to the center of the table. "We have the body of the person who did."

"We need to find out if he's really the guy," Mason added. "Naahir told us someone has been watching Jane and Annabelle for a while now."

"Naahir did this?" Aidan asked. "I knew the guy was a little off, but this?" His brows pulled together tightly when he looked at Annabelle, then me. "What does he want with the two of you?"

Kaden answered. "He doesn't want Jane or Annabelle. He wants Mason."

"Why?"

Mason sat back in his chair and crossed his arms and thrust his chin toward the window. "Because they think I might be a cure for whatever those things have."

"Because you survived a bite?" Aidan asked. "Annabelle told me about it," he answered before anyone could ask how he'd known. "You don't want to help, I'm assuming."

"You assumed wrong," Mason clipped, stunning us all.

Aidan held up his hand. "Hey, I'm sorry. Anyone would be freaking out at the thought of being poked and prodded…"

"I don't give a shit about that." Mason stood and pushed his chair under the table, his movements stiff and erratic. "Do you think I'm so selfish that I wouldn't want to help if I could?"

Aidan's voice softened, "No…"

"Okay, let's calm down," Kaden stepped in. "Why don't we…"

Whatever he was about to say was cut off by the radio crackling to life. "Report," a deep but whispered voice clipped. We all froze and stared at the radio. "Jeffery?" The voice asked again, this time his tone stronger and familiar.

Mason snatched the radio off the table. "You fucking asshole," he replied.

There was a pause, then Naahir's voice came through loud and clear. "Ah, I see you found Jeffery. May I ask what has happened to him?"

"Dead," Mason said, a chilling grin tugging his lips. "And you will be soon if you continue with this."

"Tsk, tsk, Mason. You killed one of my men? All I wanted was for you to show some compassion. Why won't you help? You could save so many lives."

"What's in it for you?"

"Besides a life free of flesh eaters? Nothing," he stated, sounding innocent. Too innocent.

When Mason didn't say anything, Naahir's voice hardened. "Don't think that just because Jeffery is dead, I don't have leverage. I have many more men ready and willing to do my bidding. You have less than twenty-four hours."

Mason threw the radio on the table, then ran his hands through his hair. "I'm going," he said to us. "I'd planned to go anyway. I'd just wanted more time." His eyes cut to mine. "But it's obvious they won't let me have it. If I leave right now, hopefully, I can get there before they try something else."

I had started shaking my head the moment his eyes had met mine and I continued to do so. *"No, you can't go. Don't give in to them,"* I signed.

"She's right. You can't give in to them," Kaden agreed.

"I see no other way." Mason's voice rose, his gaze like daggers as he glared at his friend. "I won't let them hurt her—or anyone. What they did out there," he pointed toward the window for emphasis, "was fucked up. What if they come back? What if next time their plan's not as simple as a few flesh eaters?"

I got to my feet and reached for Mason's arm, ready to tie him to the chair if I had to. He wasn't leaving. End of story. Instead, I found myself pressed against his chest, his arms solid around my middle holding me prisoner.

"That was just some passive aggressive shit," Kaden began, but Mason wasn't having it.

"And next time might be something more hands on," he interrupted.

His hold on me tightened, and I pressed my forehead to the center of his chest, dreading what he'd say next.

"I have to go. What other choice do I have?"

His statement shot a searing hot pain through my chest. Squeezing my eyes shut, I shook my head, ready to begin my objection. He couldn't leave. Not again.

"No."

Clear and unforgiving, the voice grasped my attention. I turned in Mason's arms, stunned to see Annabelle standing, her chin up and her eyes hard.

"You do have another choice," she said. *"We* have another choice. You stay. We fight."

"I can't ask you to do that," Mason replied.

"You're not asking and it's not all about you. I don't want some asshole thinking he calls the shots when it comes to *my* life. If you want to go with them, then go. But don't go because this asshole made threats. I can handle myself."

Annabelle's gaze flickered to mine before quickly looking away. "And so can Jane."

16

Mason didn't argue more after Annabelle's proclamation. He stared her down, a vein throbbing in his temple the only sign that his anger still lingered at the surface. Eventually, he sighed and agreed to think it over. His eyes, though, betrayed him. I was afraid he would do something stupid but didn't know how to stop him.

Dead tired, I pulled away, intending to head to bed. It was a wonder we were all still standing. I wasn't sure about Aidan and Annabelle, but Mason, Kaden and I had been awake for more than twenty-four hours. But Mason surprised me by scooping me in his arms, bridal style.

My breath caught in my throat and I gripped his shoulders reflexively as he swung around toward the stairs. I'd already been surrounded by his scent when he'd wrapped me in his arms, but something about being literally swept off my feet caused both of those things to intensify.

I could feel my brain begin to shut off as my exhaustion warred with longing to physically connect myself to him. To both of them. I looked over Mason's shoulder to see Kaden's intense gaze set on me.

With the last of my wits, I glanced past him, wanting to catch Annabelle's eye, hoping to express my regret once more. But my friend wasn't looking my way and my heart sank. Would she forgive me?

As soft kiss was placed on my forehead, I closed my eyes and pushed those feelings away for now. Instead, I allowed Mason and Kaden to take me to bed. There would be plenty of time for more apologies after I'd slept. I had a feeling I'd need my strength for all of the groveling.

The three of us were quiet as we entered my bedroom. I hadn't had to tell them where to go, or offer an invitation to join me. It was just assumed that we'd be sleeping together. Even if it was just sleeping. And I was totally okay with that assumption. But as Mason set me on my feet next to the bed, I gazed into his eyes, getting lost in the dark brown depths, and I no longer felt like sleeping. I wanted him. I wanted both of them. I wanted to give them a reason to stay with me. I wanted... I just wanted, period.

Kaden whipped off his shirt, the move grasping my attention. Especially when so much skin was revealed. When I licked my lips his expression went from tired to starving. It was exactly how I felt.

Mason's hands joined mine as I stripped off my clothes. Then I was reaching for him, sliding my fingers under his shirt and up his chest. He ripped the shirt off while I placed a kiss on his collarbone, letting my lips glide across to the other side. His moan vibrated beneath my palms as I slid them down to the waistband of his shorts. I followed them to the floor, landing on my knees with a soft thump, my lips never breaking away from his skin. I kissed one thigh then the other before nudging his arousal with my nose.

When he chuckled darkly, I looked up from under my lashes. Then I cupped him in my hand and wrapping my mouth around the broad tip of him. His laugh ended abruptly, turning into a groan, and his head fell back as I slid the length of him fully into my mouth.

Too occupied, I didn't notice Kaden standing behind me. He too went to his knees, his chest warming my back. I leaned into him, but when his fingers brushed through my wet curls, I arched. My throat constricted around Mason's cock causing him to gasp and his hips to jerk forward almost gagging me.

Automatically, my knees parted and I fell into the erotic moment, my mouth sucking Mason's cock, Kaden swirling his fingers over my clit, his tongue trailing down the back of my neck as my hips rotated over his hand.

Mason's fingers tightened in my hair when I pulled away, but I wasn't done. Not by a long shot. Shifting to spread my knees wider, I looked over my shoulder at Kaden. His eyes blazed a path from my face down to my toes. His tongue slowly skimmed over his bottom lip, like he was biding his time before devouring me whole. I shivered in anticipation.

"Nightstand," I signed.

He pulled a condom out of the top drawer, his eyebrows lifting when he looked back at me. Though he made no comment nor did he waste any more time before ripping open the package and sliding the condom over his thick length. Then he positioned himself on his knees behind me so I straddled him.

"Like this?" He gripped my hips and lowered me on to his cock.

For a moment, I closed my eyes and enjoyed the feel of him entering me. Stretching me. Filling me with more than just his cock. He and Mason made me feel something I'd never felt before. Peace. And along with it came Love with a capital L.

Love?

The word scared the hell out of me, but I couldn't deny it any longer. I loved them. I loved both of them more than I thought I was capable of loving anyone who wasn't my family. But not only did I love them, but I was one hundred and ten percent certain they loved me back. I had been wrong. So fucking wrong. This *thing* between the three us wasn't just loneliness and lust. It was so much more, and I couldn't lie to myself anymore.

I held back the emotional tears, but couldn't help but tighten my grip on Mason. He brushed my hair gently away from my face and met my wide-eyed gaze with a softer version of his own, showing me exactly what I'd realized.

Deepening the moment, Kaden leaned over to whisper in my ear, his warm breath causing my skin to prickle with awareness.

"I love you, Jane."

I gasped as I was pressed down fully onto his cock. He pulsed inside me and his grip tightened on my waist, encouraging me to move but I was enjoying the moment. The declaration along with the feel of him inside me.

The wet tip of Mason's cock brushed my lips and I opened my eyes to see Mason grinning above me. My nails were digging into his thighs, but instead of letting go, I tightened my grip and smiled.

"God, that smile," he said. "So wicked."

I opened my mouth to flick the tip of him with my tongue. His eyes flashed and he groaned, his fingers tightening in my hair as he pushed himself into my mouth.

Kaden used his free hand to rub my clit while urging me to move. My eyes rolled back, the pleasure so intense I stopped breathing.

The time for teasing had ended. We were seized by hunger and nothing but our love could sate us.

17

THE ROOM BLURRED AS I BLINKED RAPIDLY, TOO TIRED to hold my eyelids open. Something had woken me. The bed had jostled. A thought lingered in the back of mine, telling me I should wake up. That it was something important.

Cool air moved over my back and I shivered, snuggling closer to Kaden's chest, wishing Mason would spoon behind me again. That lingering memory returned, making me restless, but it was fleeting and it floated away as soon as something soft rested against my back.

With a contented sigh, I drifted back to sleep, happy to be warm again.

I stared at the imprint where Mason's body had once lain, spooning at my back, and felt real anger towards him. He'd left. Not only had he left, but he'd left without so much as a goodbye, sneaking off while Kaden and I had slept. Mason had done what he had chastised me for. How long ago had that been? Three days?

I looked to the window where morning was just turning the sky from inking black to soft gray. The three of us had spent the previous day and night making love, dozing off and on in between. We'd talked a little, when we'd been coherent enough, about our lives before. I'd told them about my teaching job and about my mom and dad. Kaden talked more about his niece. And of course, out of the three of us, Mason had talked the most.

"I don't have any family," he'd told me. This was something Kaden had already known, and he'd been quiet as Mason revealed a little about his life. I'd listened, absorbing all I could, wanting to know everything about both him and Kaden.

"My parents gave me up for adoption when I was born," he'd continued. "Football kept me out of trouble and was the only way I was able to afford college. My uncle, the one that owned this house? Wasn't really my uncle. Not by blood. He was my high school football coach. He took me in when I turned eighteen and the state no longer would house me."

"What happened to him?" I'd asked.

"He died of a heart attack. I'd been down here for the funeral when the world went haywire. When Kaden called to warn me, I knew this would be the perfect place to set up. Uncle Jay was a bit of a prepper."

"If only you'd stayed put like I'd told you," Kaden had added dryly.

Mason had chuckled. "Right. And leave my best friend to fend for himself? Not likely."

Kaden had snorted but said nothing more. I got the

impression the conversation had been one they'd had multiple times.

I'd thought about what he'd said. That he'd had no family. That wasn't true.

"We're your family," I'd told him.

After a long, lingering kiss, he'd whispered, "Thank you," against my lips. Then he'd taken my mouth once again, leading us down the path to more love making.

I should have been suspicious. Not because of the kiss or the lovemaking. But thinking back, I remembered his eyes. His face and the shadow that taken permanent residents over his expression since we'd entered the bedroom.

I clenched my fists at my sides and looked at the still sleeping Kaden. One of his arms spread across the bed, palm open as if he were reaching for me. Part of me wanted to succumb to his subconscious demand and scrawl back into bed with him.

Instead, I packed my things as silently as I could, debating whether or not I should wake him. Would he try to stop me from following Mason? Try to convince me it was best to stay and wait? I couldn't do that.

The decision was taken out of my hands when just as I slung the bag over my shoulders, he stirred. He patted the empty space beside him and finding no one there, sat up suddenly, his head turning one way then the other as he searched the room. His wide stare found me and his chest rose and fell with his sigh of relief.

Sliding his feet to the floor, Kaden stood from the bed. My gaze raked over his naked form from head to toe. No matter how distressed or angry, I couldn't help but appreciate the sight of him. So hard in all the right places.

"What's going on?"

He bent to rummage around in his duffle bag, finding a pair of sweat pants and pulling them on. They had moved their bags into my room the day before, and I waited for him to notice Mason's was now missing.

He looked around the room before he brought he leveled his gaze with mine. Then I knew. He'd known.

"He's gone," I signed.

"I know," he confirmed. "And you're going after him."

It wasn't a question so I didn't answer.

His jaw muscle jumped as he stalked toward me, his narrowed gaze blazing. When his chest brushed mine, I titled my chin up to hold his stare. I wasn't afraid of him. I never had been. His posturing only aroused me. My nails dug sharply into my palms, but I lost the fight, reaching for him with greedy fingers. He wrapped his arms around me and pulled me against him.

"He wanted me to promise him that I would stay here, with you. But I knew I couldn't keep that promise. I knew you wouldn't stay once you found out he'd left. Wherever you go, Jane, you're not leaving without me. Not again," he growled.

His eyes sparkled as the rising sunlight burst through the window, and for the first time since he woke I got a good look at him. He was angry that I was going to leave without him. I had assumed that from his stiff posture, but what I was just noticing was the vulnerability hiding behind that anger. He was right. I couldn't leave without him. Not just for his sake, but for mine as well.

When I nodded, a small smile split his lips before he brought them down on mine. I was just melting into the toe curling kiss when he pulled away with a smirk.

By the time my wits returned, he'd finished getting dressed.

"Come on, then." He lifted his bag and threw it over one shoulder. "With Mason's head start, we have a lot of catching up to do."

"Not that much catching up," a voice startled me.

My eyes widened at the sight of Annabelle and Aidan standing at the bedroom door. Both were dressed in outdoor clothing that included their weapons and holding their backpacks.

"I saw Mason leave about two hours ago," Annabelle continued.

I could still see her anger at me lingering, though her gaze had softened considerably.

"We're in this together," she said to me. "But Aidan and I are a package deal now. If you can't handle that, then we don't go."

I wanted to hug her, to wrap my arms around her and make her see how much she meant to me. Instead, I crossed my arms and gave her a nod of understanding.

Kaden gave them both a considering look before leveling his gaze on Aidan. "Sure you want to do this? You don't even know Mason?"

"I go wherever Anabelle goes."

Though I felt like he wanted to say more, Aidan stopped there.

Kaden thought this over for a moment before nodding. "Well, standing around is only putting us further behind. So, if you're coming, let's go."

I looked to Aidan, then Annabelle, hoping my expression displayed the full amount of regret I felt. *"You don't have to go with us,"* I signed.

"I know," Annabelle replied. "But like I said, we're in this together."

She wouldn't listen to another protest from me, and

Kaden didn't want to linger any longer. The four of us, plus Poco, left the cottage in a hurry.

Large flakes of snow slapped at the windshield as Kaden drove up the winding dirt driveway one last time, and I couldn't help but send a longing glance over my shoulder. This cottage had been my safe haven. My home. But after having Kaden and Mason back in my life, even if only briefly, I couldn't imagine staying there without them.

Kaden glanced my way then back to the road. "We'll find him, Jane. I promise."

I acknowledged the promise with a small nod, confident we would find him. Because I wouldn't rest until we not only found Mason, but made sure him, Kaden, Annabelle, and Aidan all got back home safe.

I reached for Kaden's hand to grip it tightly in my lap as I stared out the windshield. Even if Kaden failed, it was a promise I was certain to keep. Whether I was with them in the end or not.

C.E. BLACK

is a Maggie Award Winning Author in Paranormal Romance. She self-published her first book in 2011 and has since published several novels, novellas, and short stories in the Paranormal, Fantasy, and Sci-Fi Romance genres. Though steamy romance, hunky heroes, and feisty heroines are C.E.'s specialty, she enjoys surprising her readers with action-filled plots and exciting twists that make for a fast-paced read.

Her official website is www.ceblack.org.